"I'll miss you, Bethany."

He glanced away, as if fearing her rejection. She ought to nip things in the bud, but the truth was, she'd miss him, too. He'd sneaked in under her radar and stolen a piece of her heart. But like all the others she'd befriended or cared about, he'd be leaving—soon. Still, she couldn't lie to him. "I'll miss you, too."

His hopeful gaze swerved back to hers. His lips tilted upward, and he slid his hand across the table. Hers moved forward to meet his, as if it had a mind of its own. He clutched it tight. "So. . .what are we going to do about this?"

She shrugged and pulled her hand back. "Nothing."

VICKIE McDONOUGH believes God is the ultimate designer of romance. She is a wife of thirty-four years, mother to four sons, and a doting grandma. When not writing, she enjoys reading, watching movies, and traveling. Visit Vickie's Web site at www.vickiemcdonough.com

Books by Vickie McDonough

HEARTSONG PRESENTS

A Wagonload of Trouble

Vickie McDonough

Heartsong Presents

This book is dedicated to Mike and Kathleen Rasco. They've been our closest friends for as long as I can remember and are a very kind and generous couple. My husband, Robert, and I have laughed with them, gone to myriad dinners and movies together, and Kathleen and I enjoy beating Robert and Mike at Canasta and board games. Good friends are a blessing from God, and I thank Him for bringing Mike and Kathleen into our lives.

A note from the Author:
I love to hear from my readers! You may correspond with me by writing:

Vickie McDonough
Author Relations
PO Box 721
Uhrichsville, OH 44683

ISBN 978-1-60260-520-6

A WAGONLOAD OF TROUBLE

All of the characters and events in this book are fictitious. Any resemblance to actual persons, living or dead, or to actual events is purely coincidental.

Our mission is to publish and distribute inspirational products offering exceptional value and biblical encouragement to the masses.

PRINTED IN THE U.S.A.

"I'm sorry, ma'am, but there are not sufficient funds in your account to cash this check."

Bethany Schaffer stared at the young female teller, confusion clouding her mind. Why would her father send her a check for traveling expenses back home if there was no money in the ranch account? And how could that be? The dark-eyed bank clerk handed back her check and a receipt with the balance of the account imprinted on it then glanced down at the counter and fiddled with a pen.

Bethany stared at the paper. *$56.38? There's no way this can be right.*

She glanced up at the teller. "Are you certain you entered the correct account number? For Moose Valley Ranch? I'm Bethany Schaffer, and my father owns the ranch."

The woman nodded. "I'm sure, but I can check again if you'd like."

"Yes. Please do."

The teller tapped on her keyboard, her lips pursed. A few seconds later, she turned the monitor so Bethany could read it.

As if she'd jumped into a frigid lake in late December, a cold numbness seeped through her. She double-checked the name at the top of the screen and the account number. How could the ranch's balance be so low? Dad hadn't mentioned any financial troubles, and there had been at least forty thousand dollars last time she checked the account. Her dad had never been great with numbers, but to allow that bank account to get so low—it didn't make sense. Could something be wrong with him? Bethany thanked the teller then turned away, still trying to make sense of the account balance. The ranch had been through many hard times in the eighty years her family had owned it, but to be scraping the bottom of the barrel. . .

She stuck the useless check and her ID back into her purse. She hadn't even planned to cash it, but a nail in her tire had caused an added expense on the way home. She walked over to the ATM, pulled out her debit card, and made a withdrawal from her personal account so that she'd have enough cash to fill her gas tank and make it to the ranch. Then she returned to her Jeep.

Her father sure had some explaining to do. How could he have used up so much money? Had there been some big emergency that he hadn't told her about? As long as she'd been old enough to help with the bookkeeping, Moose Valley's balance had never even been close to zero.

Concern battled irritation. Bethany popped the Jeep into gear, squealing the tires as she pulled out of the parking lot. She'd wanted to leave Moose Valley Ranch and its boring life in the Upper Wind River valley of western Wyoming, and she had. She slapped the steering wheel and pulled into the gas station. Her heart suddenly constricted. Had Dad called her home to tell her he was bankrupt? Could they lose the ranch?

The ranch had been the only home she'd known until she had gone away to college. As much as she had wanted to leave, she hated the thought of not having a home to return to. She studied the small town as she pumped the gas. In the four years that she'd been attending college in Denver, little had changed. Many of the old, familiar businesses were still there behind the Old West storefront facades, but new ones had also sprung up in the scenic tourist town. With the badlands to the east and mountain peaks surrounding the town on the west, south, and north, there were endless things for visitors to see and do.

Bethany rubbed the back of her neck and stuck the nozzle back into the gas pump. Her family's guest ranch was just one that competed against many others for the tourist dollars that saw them through the long winters. Why, she couldn't begin to count the number of trail rides she'd led or accident-prone greenhorns she'd doctored.

But she'd hoped all that was in her past.

She paid the clerk inside the store and headed back to her Jeep. In just three weeks she would start working as an accountant for a big manufacturing plant in Denver. She'd have health insurance and benefits. She had less than a month to get things straightened out at the ranch so that she was free to begin her new life.

She started up the engine. Yep, just three weeks. Then she could kiss the Wyoming wilderness good-bye and return to the big city and all its amenities. Her thoughts traveled back to the bank account as she pulled onto the highway. Her stomach swirled as her mind was assaulted with concerns. What could have happened at the ranch to deplete their whole bank account? Why hadn't her dad called her sooner? What if she couldn't fix the problems in such a short time?

❧

Evan Parker leaned toward his computer monitor and maneuvered the tiny video game character—a character who looked amazingly like himself—through a maze of challenging hazards and over a hill to a tree abounding in colorful fruits labeled with the names of the fruits of the Spirit. The little man leaped up and plucked an apple labeled LOVE off a branch and dropped it into the basket that sat under the tree. The counter at the top of the screen added another 100 points to his score. The character snagged another fruit marked PATIENCE.

"C'mon, keep going. Don't crash on me now." He jiggled

the game controller, and the man grabbed a rotten apple and yanked it off the tree. A spiraling sound echoed from the speakers, and the monitor screen went blank. Evan flopped back in his office chair, the weight of his body sending it rolling backward. *Not again.*

"See, I told you the game was still crashing at that spot," said Ben Walker, a member of the game design team, through the speaker phone. "Several of the programmers here at headquarters looked at it, but they can't find the problem."

"I've redone the code on that section three times, but I must have missed something. I'll have another look at it after dinner." Evan rolled his head around to work the kinks out of his neck, leaned back in his chair, and looked at the ceiling of his home office. He needed to get past this problem and work on the next section of the Christian video game he was helping design. He had to succeed. His dream was riding on this.

"Hey, sweat not," Ben said, "we're a little ahead of schedule."

"Thanks. Listen, I'm having dinner at my sister's house tonight, so I've got to go." Evan started the shutdown on his computer and turned off his monitor.

"Mmm. . .home-cooked food. Lucky you. I'm having my usual three-course microwave supper tonight. Talk to you tomorrow."

The line went dead, and Evan clicked off his phone. He ought to be working tonight, but Erin had wooed him with not just one of his favorites—chicken and dumplings—but also with butterscotch pie.

What could his sister want to talk about that required her to make two of his favorite foods? He searched his mind, trying to remember if she'd mentioned something to him before about watching the kids or doing a job he'd forgotten about, but he drew a blank.

He took a quick shower then gelled his short hair, raking his fingers through it until it looked passable. He rubbed his hand over his five o'clock shadow. "Better to skip shaving than be late to dinner, dude."

He grabbed a shirt off the back of a kitchen chair and sniffed to make sure it was still clean. Five minutes later he was on his way. As he drove past the quiet University of Wyoming campus, he felt his tense neck and shoulder muscles begin to relax. "No classes to teach this summer. No, sir."

No more lesson plans to prepare or projects or papers to grade. He turned the vehicle onto Erin's street, grinning. And if things went as planned, he'd never have to go back to teaching. Not that teaching was bad, but he wanted more freedom with his schedule—and landing the gaming contract was just what he needed.

He stopped at a red light. In the two weeks since the spring semester had ended, he'd gotten quite a bit of programming done on the video game. Not as much as he'd hoped, but at least he wasn't behind schedule.

Five minutes later he pulled into Erin's driveway. But his ten-year-old nephew didn't come flying out the door upon Evan's arrival like he usually did. He climbed out of his new hybrid SUV and beeped the lock and alarm on the remote then ran his hand along the blue paint, marveling at the fact that he'd finally purchased his dream machine. As he walked up the driveway, he noted again that Erin's house needed to be painted. Somehow he'd have to squeeze in time for that while the weather was warm.

He stepped into the modest home that smelled like fresh-cooked chicken. His stomach growled, and he was glad that he'd taken the time to come. He crossed through the entryway and noted the empty kitchen. The pot on the stove beckoned him, and he couldn't resist swiping his finger along the top and sticking it into his mouth. "Mmm. Awesome!"

"It's not the same, Mom. He'll ruin everything." Taylor's loud voice reverberated down the short hallway.

What had Jamie done to upset the finicky fourteen-year-old girl now? Evan wanted his own kids one day but wouldn't mind if they could just skip the whole teen scene. Being a single mother, Erin had her hands full and didn't need Taylor acting up. He could hear Erin's soft, patient voice replying to Taylor but couldn't make out the words.

"But, Mo—om. He's such a geek."

Ouch! Geek didn't begin to describe sports-minded Jamie, so Taylor must have been upset about someone else. He didn't know whom Taylor referred to, but he felt sorry for the guy. He returned to the kitchen and set the table. What was so bad about being a geek anyway?

Footsteps echoed behind him, and he glanced over his shoulder. His sister's lips were pressed into a thin line, but her blue eyes lit when she saw him. "Hey! I didn't hear you come in."

"I get to sneak bites that way." He grinned.

Erin looked at the pot on the stove, where its lid sat crooked. "You did steal a bite, you rascal."

Evan held up his hands. "Guilty as charged."

His sister pulled down three bowls. "Jamie isn't eating. He's got chicken pox." The last word came out on a sigh.

"That stinks." Evan scratched his arm and then crinkled his brow. Two days ago he and Jamie had been roughhousing, and he'd seemed fine then. Evan sure didn't need to get sick this summer with all he had to do. "Have I had them?"

"Yeah, we both have. Although, if I remember correctly, you only had a very mild case. Taylor had them in kindergarten, so she's safe. Don't you remember how she cried when she missed so much school that fall? Oh, how times change." Erin shook her head. She pulled the lid off the chicken and dumplings, and the kitchen filled with the fragrant scent, making Evan's mouth water as she dished up the three bowls. Erin added a scoop of green peas to each bowl and set them on the table. "Taylor, dinner's ready."

Evan fixed two glasses of water and one of milk for Taylor and set them beside the bowls; then he took his spot at the head of the table. He didn't like sitting in the place that had belonged to Erin's ex-husband, but the small table only had four places, and that was Evan's regular spot.

Taylor stomped into the kitchen, gave him the evil eye, and slumped onto her chair. She crossed her arms and stared at her cup. "I hate milk."

Evan lifted one eyebrow. "Since when?"

Taylor rolled her eyes. "Since like forever."

He resisted responding. It would only make things worse. For as long as he could remember, Taylor had loved milk. Everything about her was changing. The sweet, happy girl he'd played board games with had morphed into a snobbish teenager with a bad attitude.

He grabbed her cup and swapped it with his.

"Hey!" Taylor scowled.

"Hey what? You said you hated milk, so I graciously traded with you."

The teen looked as if she wanted to argue, but he had her, and she knew it. Erin sat down and made eye contact with him, letting him know not to encourage Taylor. He crossed his arms over his chest. "I'm only trying to keep her happy."

Looking tired, Erin bowed her head. "Just pray. Please."

With dumplings awaiting, he made short work of the prayer and picked up his spoon. "Mmm-mmm. Delicious as always."

"It's a bribe," Taylor spouted then filled her mouth.

Evan didn't want to examine what she meant and quickly devoured his meal. With his stomach warm and nearly full, he leaned one arm over the back of his chair. "Too bad Jamie got sick with summer just starting. Guess that means he won't be going on that wagon train trip with you."

Erin set her spoon down and stared at him.

Uh-oh. He knew that look. "I can't watch him. You know I have to finish that video game by mid-August, plus, what do I know about caring for a sick kid?"

Taylor snorted, and Erin's mouth twisted in a wry grimace. He looked from mother to daughter. What had he missed?

"You're not getting off that easy." Taylor grabbed the glass of milk and gave him back his water.

"I thought you hated that."

Taylor shrugged. "It goes good with this meal."

Erin stood and collected the bowls, took them to the sink, and filled them with water. She pulled the pie from the fridge and set it on the counter. All manner of thoughts raced through his mind. Could he watch Jamie and still do his work? Erin lifted a fat golden triangle topped with white meringue, and his mouth watered.

His sister didn't have an Internet hookup. After dealing with her husband's pornography problem, she refused to have online service, even though Taylor constantly complained that it made doing her schoolwork more difficult. Maybe if Jamie wasn't hurling all the time, he could stay at Evan's house. He scratched his neck. Did kids hurl when they had the chicken pox?

His sister set a heaping slice of butterscotch pie in front of him, and he picked up his fork. His mother's recipe was the best he'd ever eaten. He closed his eyes and let the sweet caramel flavor tease his senses. Maybe if he agreed to watch his nephew, she'd send the rest of the pie home with him. He didn't mind eating pie for breakfast, lunch, and dinner.

Erin cleared her throat and glanced at Taylor. Evan realized that neither had taken a bite of her dessert.

"Just tell him, Mom, and get it over with." Taylor sighed and rolled her eyes again. "This really stinks."

Erin heaved a sigh. "I need to ask a big favor of you."

Here it comes. "Well. . .shoot."

"Since Jamie is sick, we can't go with Taylor on the wagon train trip we've planned for all year. Jamie is heartbroken. I want to know if you'll go with Taylor." She turned her fork facedown and then faceup, over and over, but didn't look at him.

Evan let the words process in his mind for a minute. She wasn't asking him to watch Jamie—and he'd nearly had that all worked out in his head. She wanted him to leave Laramie and drive out west toward the Tetons—out in the sticks.

Nobody said a word. They all knew it took him time to process a decision like this. Taylor wolfed down her pie, but Erin didn't touch hers. Evan felt his eyes widen. She was asking him to go on a two-week wagon ride in the wilds of Wyoming. Him, a bona fide geek, who hated bugs, snakes—nature—and had hardly traveled anywhere. "You can't be serious."

"See?" Taylor curled her lip at him. "I told you he wouldn't do it. He's such a nerd."

"Taylor. That's no way to talk about your uncle, especially after all he's done for us."

"Well, it's the truth." She flung down her fork and stood. "Just cancel the whole trip. I didn't want to go anyway."

Numb to her insult because it was the truth, Evan watched his niece stomp out of the room.

"She doesn't mean that." Erin sighed and pushed her uneaten pie toward the center of the table. "You know how her American history class at school worked the whole year to raise money for this trip, and she can't go without an adult escort. I wouldn't ask you to go, but Taylor has had her heart set on this for so long. It's the only thing I've seen her excited about since Clint left. I can't go because I need to be here to care for Jamie."

"I could keep Jamie." How did he go from *No way am I watching Jamie* to acquiescing? It was the lesser evil, that's how.

"You wouldn't know what to do to make him comfortable. He'd be complaining and bugging you all the time to play video games and keeping you from your work."

Evan leaned forward, elbows on the table. "And how will I work if I go into the high country? They probably don't even have Internet at this place—what's it called?"

"Moose Valley Ranch, and I'm sure they do since they have a Web site with an e-mail link. I know it's a lot to ask, but it's only two weeks. It would do you good to get outside and get some sun."

"So it's about me now?" Evan stood and took his plate and cup to the sink. "Besides, I get sun every morning when I go jogging."

"Sorry, I didn't mean to lay a guilt trip on you, but this trip wasn't cheap. You know the jillions of fund-raisers Taylor did. You contributed to all of them, and I've saved for a year because Taylor wanted to go so badly."

"Can't you get a refund?"

"Maybe. I don't know." Erin threw up her hands and sighed. "I don't want Taylor to be disappointed. She's had so few things to smile about lately. Besides"—Erin looked to the left and right then leaned forward, her expression pleading—"I need a break from her," she whispered then looked at the ground. "I know that sounds horrible, but it's true."

Evan felt as cornered as his video character when it had stumbled into Daniel's lions' den after making a wrong move. Without Daniel's level of faith, his character hadn't survived. Evan wanted to help his sister and niece, but could he give up two weeks and still finish his project on time? Maybe he could work on the game in his free time, and if the guest ranch had Internet access, he could still turn in his progress reports and contact the others on his team if he had a question. "When is this trip?"

His sister's lips pursed, and she seemed to be studying something fascinating on the wall. "Uh. . .ten days from now."

Evan's eyes widened, then he schooled his expression. *When* didn't really matter. Anytime this summer was a bad time. Erin didn't know he wanted to quit teaching and work permanently from home for the computer company so that he'd have more time to help her out with the kids. There was no way of escape without disappointing someone. It might as well be himself. "All right, I'll do it."

Erin's tense expression morphed into a smile that made him glad he'd agreed. He'd have to remember that grin when he was knee-deep in wildflowers and bugs, and stuck with a cranky teenager with a Teton-size attitude.

two

A familiar warmth tugged at Bethany's heart as she drove up the mile-long dirt road leading to the main lodge of Moose Valley Ranch. Home. So familiar, but so vastly different from the city where she now lived. An array of wildflowers painted the meadow on her left yellow and white, while conifers, aspens, and lodgepole pines rose up on her right, creating a natural windbreak. She hadn't been back to Moose Valley since last year's Christmas holiday. She should have come home on spring break, but instead she'd gotten a job and worked. The excuse had felt legitimate at the time. Rolling her head, she tried to work loose her tight shoulder muscles.

"Why should I feel guilty? Wasn't that the whole reason for going to college?" *So I could get an education and support myself—and leave Moose Valley behind?*

If nothing else, she should have returned sooner just to see her dad. But it wasn't as if he were all alone. Anywhere from six to twelve employees helped with cleaning the guest cabins, cooking, caring for the horses, and managing the wagon tours and trail rides. Bethany heaved a sigh and honked her horn at the small herd of Black Angus moseying across the dirt road. Leaning out her window, she yelled, "C'mon. Move it."

Taking out her frustrations on dumb cattle and rationalizing that her dad had plenty of help didn't drive away her guilt. The bottom line was that she had neglected him. If only he'd step into the twenty-first century; then she could have e-mailed him. A lot of good it did to have a Web site for the ranch and e-mail contact if he wouldn't learn to use it. Maybe he'd be more willing once she hooked up the new state-of-the-art computer she'd brought home with her.

As the last calf bawled and trotted after its mother, Bethany pounded her fist on the steering wheel and stepped on the gas. She topped the final hill, and Moose Valley spread out before her, mountains jutting up high on her left and in front of her, and the forest on her right. The sight certainly was magnificent and rivaled anything Colorado had to offer. So why wasn't she content to stay here?

Shaking off her nostalgic melancholy, she sped down the dirt road and parked in front of the main lodge. The near-empty parking lot, which should have been packed with the vehicles of summer visitors, captured her attention. Where were all the cars? Summer was their busy season—the time they earned enough money to run on the rest of the year. Trying not to worry, she slipped out of the Jeep, lips pursed, and jogged up the steps to the main entrance.

Inside, nothing had changed. The woodlands decor of the three-story building was the same, but no one stood at the registration desk to welcome her. Maggie Holmes had occupied that job last summer and was supposed to be back this year. "Hellooo. . .Maggie? Dad?"

No reply. "Weird." Bethany slipped behind the counter and into the back office. Her father sat at his desk, one hand forked into his hair, studying a ledger book. She didn't want to startle him, so she edged beside him, shuffling her shoes.

He lowered his hand and looked up at her, his dark eyes staring blankly for a moment. Then he blinked and suddenly focused on her. A smile tugged at his lips. "Beth, you're home. At last."

He stood, and she fell into his arms, just as she'd done so many times before. Why had she stayed away so long?

After a warm moment, she stepped back, crossed her arms, and leaned against the desk. "So. . .where's Maggie, and why is the bank account so low?"

A smile tilted one corner of her dad's mouth. "Always one to get right to the point, huh?"

Bethany shrugged. "And while we're at it, why aren't there many cars in the lot? I thought we were booked solid for the summer."

Rob Schaffer ran a hand through his thick silver hair, which contrasted nicely with his Wyoming sun-baked skin. Tiny lines crinkled in the corners of his dark brown eyes, and she realized for the first time that he was starting to age. When had that happened?

He sighed and dropped back into his chair.

She lowered her hip to the side of his desk. "You told me last time I talked to you that we had a full slate of customers lined up—even had to turn some folks away."

He fiddled with a pen but didn't look up at her. "We were booked solid, but the past couple of weeks a lot of people have called and canceled their reservations. Almost like an epidemic. I don't know if it has to do with the economy or something else."

He ran his hand through his hair. "I had to refund so many deposits that I had to let some of the workers go." He glanced up, then his gaze darted away. "Maggie, too."

Bethany felt her eyes widen. They had never laid off employees before. "How many?"

He huffed a sigh so heavy that it fluttered the papers on the desk. "Eight."

She tried to wrap her mind around how they could function with so few remaining workers. She stood and paced to the wall that held pictures of past guests then turned and walked the few feet to the other wall. "What about the customers who came the past few weeks? What happened to their payment money?"

"Bills. Payroll. You know the routine. I'm sorry you had to come home and find things in such a mess. Your mother never would have let things get like this." He rubbed his hand across his jaw. "I know you're planning to start work at that new job soon, but I didn't know what else to do except to call you home. I can't run this place by myself anymore and tend to the cattle, too."

Concern washed over Bethany in waves, mixing with the confusing thoughts assaulting her. Was he sick? Was the ranch too much work now that he was getting older? "Dad, you're not sick, are you?"

His head jerked up, eyes wide. "No, of course not."

She eyed him, but he looked sincere. "Are we in any danger of losing the ranch?"

He shook his head. "The ranch has been paid off for years, but things may be lean for a while."

Bethany flipped through the pages of the receipts ledger. Income was definitely down. "I don't understand. We had plenty of money in the bank when I left here at Christmas. What happened to it all?"

Her father looked away. A muscle in his jaw tightened.

"Dad?"

"I suppose you'll find out anyway." He glanced up and stood. "I probably should have just made payments, but I wanted to get those loans off my books and off my shoulders." He looked out the office door as if gathering his courage then faced her again. "It went to pay off your college loans."

Her head swirled with thoughts as she tried to grasp what he'd said. He'd paid off her student loans? She'd never asked him to cover them. She'd planned to pay them off herself. Sure, it would take a while, but she'd get it done. But now there were no loans, only a ranch—a family legacy—on the brink of financial disaster. The floor seemed to shift under her. Bethany reached out to a nearby bookcase to steady herself.

The deplorable state of the ranch's finances was all her fault?

❧

Evan eased up on the gas and guided the SUV around a pothole the size of his bathtub. He'd saved for years to buy his new vehicle, and he wasn't going to ruin it driving on a gravel road at a ridiculous speed just to please his niece.

"We'll never get there at this rate." Taylor stared out her window, arms crossed, and slouched back in the seat. "I don't know why we couldn't have caravanned with my class."

"We should be there any time now, and then you can see your friends. The sign where we turned off said it was just another mile."

They crested a hill, and an eye-catching valley spread out before them. He wanted to take a moment to savor the panoramic view, but he had a restless teenager prodding him on. He steered the SUV toward the largest building, an Alpine lodge with a parking lot out front. A sign identified the place as the dining hall and registration building. He parked, climbed out, and looked around as he stretched the kinks out of his stiff back. A large barn sat off to his left with tall mountain peaks jutting up behind it. As much as he'd dreaded coming on this trip, he had to admit the place looked like it was straight out of an Old West movie, all except for the alpine architecture.

"Nice, huh?" Taylor stopped beside him and leaned against the SUV.

"Yep. Not as rustic as I'd expected." Evan glanced at her, hoping the snaps on the back of her jeans didn't scratch his paint.

"Should we unload?"

He shook his head. "Let's check-in first. We may not be staying in this building."

Taylor used her foot to push away from the vehicle, and Evan winced. He followed her up the steps and into the lodge. Fragrant scents of something cooking greeted them.

"Too cool! Look at that moose head." She pointed over the registration desk. "You think they shot that here? I wonder if we'll see a live moose."

Evan shrugged. A pretty blond walked through a door behind the counter and smiled.

"Welcome to Moose Valley Ranch. I'm Bethany Schaffer."

Evan held out his hand. Warm brown eyes captured his and sent his pulse skyrocketing. The woman's honey blond hair draped around her shoulders in pleasant waves. She scowled, and Taylor nudged him in the side. He realized he still held the woman's hand and released it.

"And you would be?" Miss Schaffer's brow lifted, making those chocolate eyes look larger.

Taylor cleared her throat. "I'm Taylor Anderson, and this is my uncle, Evan Parker. I'm part of the Oak Hill Junior High class."

Evan shifted his feet. He should have introduced himself instead of letting Taylor do it, but his tongue didn't want to work for some strange reason. Must be the fresh mountain air.

Miss Schaffer pulled out a thick ledger book and ran her finger down a list of names. "I have a reservation for an Erin, Jamie, and Taylor Anderson, but not a Mr. Parker." She looked up without raising her head.

Evan forced his voice into action. "Erin's my sister, but she had to stay home with my nephew—Jamie—who has chicken pox."

"Hmm. . .well, that may create a problem."

Evan's gaze wandered to the huge moose head on the wall behind the counter; then the woman's words registered. "What kind of problem?"

Miss Schaffer straightened and tapped her pencil on the counter. "Miss Anderson requested a single room with a king-size bed and a rollaway. I assume you would prefer a room of your own rather than sharing one with your niece. Am I wrong?"

He digested her words and suddenly realized what she meant. Heat warmed his face as he thought of sharing a single room with his cantankerous niece. He wouldn't get a lick of work done, not to mention it didn't seem proper. "Uh. . .do you have a two-bedroom suite by chance? With wireless Internet?"

The young woman's pink lips puckered as she checked a file box filled with colored index cards. "I have a two-bedroom cabin available with a kitchenette. It doesn't have Internet service but has a color TV. The cost is more than what you were charged for a room in our Muskrat Lodge." She waved a hand over her shoulder. "That's the wide, two-story building behind this lodge. Of course, your niece will be farther from her friends, since they're all staying at Muskrat."

Evan considered what she said. It was logical that a cabin would cost more, but since Jamie wasn't here, they should still get a refund. He couldn't expect full reimbursement at this late date, but surely they should grant a partial one. Maybe he could get the cabin and still get back some money for Erin. But then the cabin didn't have Internet service.

"Since my brother couldn't come, shouldn't we get back the money we paid for him? It was an awful lot." Taylor lifted her chin and boldly spouted the very words that had crossed Evan's mind, although she used less tact than he would have. She tapped her neon blue nails on the counter.

Miss Schaffer's brown eyes widened, and a look of panic

dashed across her face before she schooled her expression. She gazed at him. "Surely you can't expect a refund at this late date, Mr. Parker. We reserved a place for your nephew, and while I'm sorry that he got sick and couldn't come, it isn't our fault."

Evan straightened. He hated confrontation, but it was Erin's money that was on the line. "I think some kind of reimbursement is in order. You won't have to feed a growing adolescent."

"And can Jamie ever pack away food! Consider yourself lucky." Taylor nibbled at the nail on her index finger then looked down at it.

Myriad expressions passed over Miss Schaffer's pretty face.

"We can wait if you need to check with your supervisor," Evan said.

The woman narrowed her eyes. "I don't have a supervisor, Mr. Parker. My father and I own this facility."

Evan swallowed, feeling thoroughly put in his place. Why hadn't he considered she might live here?

Her expression softened. "How about I let you have the cabin and not charge you extra, and we'll call it even?"

Evan shook his head. "I've got to have a room with an Internet connection. Don't you have any at all? My sister said you have a Web site and e-mail address, so you have to have a Web connection somewhere."

She pursed her lips. "Part of the reason people come to Moose Valley is to get away from things like the Internet. You'll only be in your room two nights before the wagon train starts. Surely you can do without the Internet for that short amount of time."

For a resort owner, the gal sure wasn't very hospitable. Evan straightened. The fragrant aromas wafting from the direction of the dining hall tugged at his attention and made his stomach grumble. His mouth watered, but he forced his mind back to the business at hand. "I'm on a short deadline at work. I hadn't planned to make this trip, but I did it to help out my sister."

"Humph." Taylor glared at him then walked over to a rocker facing a large picture window with an inspiring view and plunked herself down.

"*And* to help my niece." Too little too late to pacify the finicky teen, but he had to make the effort. He didn't want her to think that he didn't want to be here, even though she already did.

Miss Schaffer rummaged through the file box again. The buildings at the ranch looked fairly up-to-date, but the place was so backward they hadn't even computerized their registration information. So much for twenty-first-century living. The woman pressed her lips together until they turned into a thin line. She was pretty, in an earthy way, with her sun-kissed tan and golden hair.

She looked up and caught him watching her, and her brow crinkled. "I do have a luxury suite available that has two bedrooms and Internet. It's on the second floor of this building. I suppose I could let you have it—if we called things even."

He wouldn't get any money back for Erin if he agreed. He looked around the lodge as he considered the offer. The inside was filled with thick pine furnishings with woodland animal decorations. Off to his right was a small gift shop and snack bar with a sign on the window that read Moose Valley Mercantile. The door was open and the light was on, but nobody was inside. Maybe he could get a caffeine fix in there.

Miss Schaffer cleared her throat. "Will that do, Mr. Parker?"

Taylor stopped rocking and glanced over her shoulder. "You have to give him a minute to think things through. You know that Bible verse that says to be slow to speak? Well, that was written for my uncle."

Evan scowled. She made him sound like an idiot. He couldn't help that he had to look at things from different angles before making a decision. His brain functioned more like a ten-year-old PC than one of the new quad-core processors now available on computers. Since the woman didn't seem willing to grant Erin a refund no matter what, and he did need Internet service and two bedrooms, he might as well accept the offer. It sounded like the best he was likely to get. He nodded. "All right. It's a deal."

Miss Schaffer stared at the hand he'd extended in her direction for the second time and finally reached out and shook it. Evan felt as if a power spike surged through his body at her touch, and he stared at the woman. Her curious gaze captured his; then she frowned and tugged her hand away.

"Yes. . .well. . .I'll need to make sure that suite is ready since we didn't have anyone booked in there. Let me get the key, and I'll check it while you two have a look around. Would you like to purchase a snack to eat while you wait?"

Evan looked over his shoulder at Taylor, who stood and faced him. She nodded.

"Sounds good."

They followed the young woman into the tiny store, and Evan couldn't help noticing her shapely figure and easy gait. He forced his attention on the glass refrigerator, which held a variety of pop and bottles of juice. He and Taylor each selected a can, and she snagged a candy bar while he chose a granola bar. Evan noticed several packages of computer cables hanging on the wall and selected one. Obviously, he wasn't the first to show up expecting wireless Internet. Miss Schaffer rang up their purchase, and he paid her.

"You're welcome to look in the barn, but don't handle the horses unless one of the staff is around."

He thought about his odd reaction to Miss Schaffer's touch. Though twenty-eight, he'd had few dates. Not that he didn't want to date; he'd just never met a woman who stirred his interest long enough to maintain a long-term relationship. Evan watched her turn and walk back into the other room. Her black capris and pink knit top looked out of place for a dude ranch, and she sounded well educated. Where could she have gone to college way out here? She mumbled something to an older gentleman in the office behind the counter.

The man leaned back in his chair and waved at Evan. "I'm Rob Schaffer. Welcome to Moose Valley."

Evan nodded and popped the lid of his Coke can. It hissed and sent up a sweet scent. He took a swig, and his gaze followed the young woman as she climbed the stairs to the right of the mercantile. In spite of their rocky start, Evan hoped that he might get to know Bethany Schaffer better. Not that there was any reason to. But she intrigued him. And that was enough to make him want to learn more about her.

&

"Thought you said you weren't ever going on another one of these tours." Big Jim Reynolds gave Bethany a cocky grin and stacked the last crate of supplies into the back of the ranch's Jeep.

Heat warmed her cheeks. "I know what I said. I'd hoped I'd seen my last trip, but it wasn't to be." If she didn't have to lead this tour, she'd be assembling the new computer and inputting their records onto the new accounting program she'd purchased, but that would have to wait until she returned.

Bethany slung her gear onto the back passenger seat and glanced at the crates of supplies. She'd checked through all the boxes last night and made sure they had everything on the list. She closed the side door, grateful to have the vehicle leading the way. There had been a time or two on past treks that the truck had been needed in case of an emergency. She hoped they wouldn't have to deal with anything that severe on this trip.

"Hey, kiddo."

She spun around at the sound of her father's voice. "Where are you going?"

He patted his chest pocket and smiled. "The bank. That schoolteacher gave us a nice, fat check."

"Whew! Let's not cut it so close next time."

"Hopefully, there won't be a next time."

She watched him amble to his pickup, and then she turned to study the group of guests gathered round, waiting to leave for the first day of the two-week tour. A boy who looked to be around thirteen sneaked up behind two girls and waved a lizard in their faces. The girls squealed and chased him around a parked car.

Bethany scanned the crowd of teenagers, mostly decked out in new cowboy or mountain boots, jeans, and long-sleeved shirts. Several sported fleece-lined vests or had jackets tied around their waists. It may be summer, but at an elevation of over seven thousand feet, the days could be cool and the nights just plain cold. Satisfied that everyone had complied with the rules to bring some type of outerwear, she headed for her wagon.

"You get him, Lacy," a tall boy yelled at the girls who were still trying to catch the boy with the lizard. Suddenly he stopped and turned around with the lizard pointed outward in one hand. The girls skidded to a stop on the rocky ground, screamed, and ran the other direction. A group of boys howled with laughter.

Bethany shook her head. They wouldn't be so loud and feisty tomorrow morning after the excitement wore off, their iPods had run out of power, and they grew bored with the view of the forest and mountains. It was always the same, trip after boring trip. She rubbed the back of her stiff neck. The only workers staying behind besides her dad were the dining room cook, one maid to clean the rooms of the few ranch guests not going on the wagon tour, and the ranch foreman. Never in her memory had they ever been stretched so thin.

And it was all her fault.

No, it wasn't completely her fault. Dad could have made payments on those loans or left them for her just as she'd planned. The check from the school group would help, but they weren't out of the woods yet.

Bethany crossed the graveled parking lot and examined the wagon she'd be driving. She checked the harnesses, knowing Big Jim didn't need her supervising, but it was a habit she'd formed at fifteen when she'd first helped lead tours.

"Gather around, everybody." Behind her, a woman shouted at all the school kids and their parents. "I have your wagon assignments." She rattled off a list of names, and a noisy group of adults and teens headed for the first wagon.

Bethany wasn't sure why she was relieved when Evan Parker's niece headed for the second wagon instead of the final one that Bethany would be driving, but not having to ride with the computer geek and his bad-attitude niece was fine with her. She double-checked the ties that held up the sides of the wagon's canvas top to allow their guests to enjoy the breathtaking views. The wagon creaked as it filled with passengers. The rubber tires, which provided a smoother ride, looked fully aired up. Everything was a go.

She climbed up to her bench seat and noticed a small tear in the canvas canopy. That would have to be repaired. If it got much larger, the whole wagon cover might have to be replaced. Bethany picked up the leather reins and watched the city slickers climb into wagon number two. Taylor Anderson was the last in line and chatted with another girl about the same size as her. Taylor looked over her shoulder as if searching for someone. A boy, probably. Wasn't that all most junior high girls were interested in?

Bethany had enjoyed meeting the boys who came to the ranch, but she'd never dated until she'd gone away to school. College. She exhaled a heavy sigh. If only her dad hadn't felt it necessary to pay off her college loans. She had never expected him to do so. Must go back to his heritage of caring for his own and not wanting to owe anybody anything. A man had to stand on his own two feet, he often said.

She breathed in a chest full of fresh air—so much cleaner than Denver's—and pulled her hair back, wrapped a thin elastic band around it, and stuck her hat back on. It might take her longer than she had planned to get things running smoothly again at the ranch. Would her new boss be willing to let her start a few weeks later than originally scheduled?

Big Jim stood outside the first wagon, next to the teacher who appeared to be counting heads. Her totals would have to agree with his before they took one step out of the parking lot. One of Bethany's draft horses shook his head and pawed the ground, eager to be off. The chatter level in the back of the wagon was high enough to send any country girl out into the wilderness in search of quiet. She'd learned long ago to put it out of her mind—but back then she'd been dreaming of her future away from the ranch.

"Someone's missing from this group," the teacher said. She held up her index finger and counted the people in the second wagon again and then looked at her chart. "There are only twelve in this wagon, but there should be thirteen."

Jim ambled over and counted, confirming that someone was missing.

Taylor Anderson leaned back in her seat and crossed her

arms. Now that Bethany thought of it, she hadn't seen the girl's uncle once this morning. The memory of how her heart jumped as she looked into his startling blue eyes still made her pulse kick up a notch even now. Maybe he was tall and appealing with his lightly tanned skin and messed-up hair, but he sure was an oddball. A door slammed, and a man came jogging out the front door of the main lodge. He cradled a backpack in his arms like a baby and had a sleeping bag dangling from one hand and a duffel bag hanging over one shoulder.

Bethany shook her head as Evan Parker hurried toward the group, wearing a wrinkled oxford cloth shirt, khakis, and a worn pair of tennis shoes. She shook her head. On every trip she picked out the greenest of the greenhorns, and on this trip, it was definitely Evan Parker. Oh, he was cute enough with his short brown hair sprouting in different directions as if he'd just run his hand through it and those sky blue eyes, but he was city through and through.

The teacher saw him coming and glared in his direction, but she sashayed to Bethany's wagon and started counting. Big Jim cast a glance over his wide shoulder then looked up at Bethany, brows lifted. He shook his head and seemed to be stifling a smile.

A movement near the barn snagged Bethany's attention. A familiar reddish brown Rhode Island Red rooster strutted out of the barn, as if to say he was being left behind. "You forgot Ed."

Jim shook his head. "I didn't forget him. I just didn't want to have to listen to him squawking any longer than I had to. Soon as we're done counting, I'll catch him."

Ed added a dose of realism to the trip with his early morning cock-a-doodles. Some of their patrons loved the effect while others despised the crotchety old bird. Bethany pulled her attention back to Mr. Parker. He slowed his pace as he crossed into the parking lot, a look of relief on his face.

Ed suddenly made a beeline for the man, squawking and flapping his wings. Taylor's uncle didn't see the bird, which was coming up fast behind him.

Bethany stood, hoping to stop the man from getting pecked.

"Look out!" someone yelled from the first wagon.

Mr. Parker glanced over his shoulder at the same time Ed attacked his heel. He high-stepped toward the wagon, slapping the sleeping bag at the aggressive rooster and holding his backpack tight against his chest. Bethany bit her top lip to keep from laughing, but that didn't stop the teens in the wagons. Kids leaned out from the two wagons ahead, and Bethany felt her own tip to the left as people rushed to see. Cheers erupted, for both the bird and the man.

"Oh dear. Help me up." The teacher hurried into the back of Bethany's wagon with one of the guest's assistance.

Mr. Parker glanced wide-eyed from wagon to wagon, and Bethany pointed at the one ahead of her. He pranced toward the wagon and leaped up the steps, collapsing in the seat across from Taylor.

Big Jim shook his head and grabbed the flapping rooster from behind as the laughter slowly died out. Taylor Anderson leaned back on the padded seat that ran along the right side of the wagon, looking as if she'd like to disappear. Evan Parker peered out the back of the wagon, and something like relief passed over his face when he saw Jim snag the rooster. He smiled at his niece and said something that made her roll her eyes and look away. He dropped his duffel bag to the floor and opened his backpack.

Bethany felt her eyes go wide as he pulled out a laptop. Never in all of her years at the ranch had anyone taken a computer on one of their tours. He leaned back on the seat, lifted his left ankle, and rested it on his knee. Then he set the computer on his lap, lifted the top, and waited until the screen lit up. After a few moments, his fingers zipped along at a fast pace, and the man seemed oblivious to his surroundings. What was so important on that computer that it couldn't wait for a few weeks?

She'd known the first time she saw Evan Parker that he'd most likely be the greenest of the city slickers. But not even she could have imagined this.

three

Evan pursed his lips and hit the SAVE button. His last battery pack was almost out of power, and it was better to save the work he'd just completed and shut down the system than risk running totally out of juice and losing it. The computer fan ceased blowing. He closed the lid on his laptop and looked around. When the wagons had first left the ranch yard, the noise level had been so high he'd found it difficult to work, but once in his groove, he was able to tune out everyone. Typing while riding in a jostling wagon on a rutted road had been a whole other issue.

He stretched his arms, working the kinks out of his shoulders, and smiled at Taylor. She glared at him, crossed her arms, and looked out the back of the wagon. *Uh-oh, looks like I've done something wrong. Again.* He turned sideways and stared out the back of the wagon at the amazing view. A thick forest of dark green gave way to a trio of peaks that lifted their faces high into the sky. They were so tall that they still had snow on them. Were they the Tetons? He should know.

Following his wagon, Bethany Schaffer drove the last wagon. The pretty woman leaned forward with her elbows on her knees and the reins dangling in her hands. A dark brown Western hat shaded her face, and she appeared deep in thought. He figured it didn't take much effort to drive one of the Conestoga replicas. The horses were probably used to following the wagon in front of them.

"Whoa!" a man's voice called out from somewhere up ahead. Evan's wagon slowed.

"Sure is pretty out here, isn't it, Mr. Parker?"

Evan glanced across the wagon at Mrs. James. The thirty-something brunette had been making eyes at him ever since she arrived at Moose Valley and had learned that he was single. He didn't want to encourage her but neither did he want to be rude. He shoved his laptop into the padded backpack, picked up his duffel bag, and glanced at her. "Uh. . .yeah. Real pretty."

She blushed. His gut twisted. She must have misconstrued his comment.

"What do we do now?" Mrs. James's daughter asked.

Taylor leaned forward. "I heard there was a lake we could swim in. I'm ready to get out of this wagon and do something fun."

Make that two. Evan climbed out and looked around. More than a dozen tents were mounted on wooden platforms in the grassy field. A brilliant blue lake was nestled at one end of the narrow valley and surrounded by mountains. He'd never been anywhere so. . .wild. He hugged his laptop nestled in his backpack. Surely there had to be a power source up here somewhere.

Taylor stood behind the black Jeep and waited her turn to claim her duffel bag. She smiled at Misty Chamberlain, her best friend, and Evan's heart warmed to see her happy. If not for her, he'd hightail it back to civilization.

Next month he'd be twenty-nine. On the same day, Taylor would be fifteen. She'd always been special because she'd been born on his birthday, but in the past year she'd morphed into someone he barely recognized. He hiked his duffel bag onto his shoulder. He was praying hard that this rebellious stage she was going through would be a short one.

Sighing, he watched Bethany Schaffer hop down from the wagon. She patted her team of horses and fiddled with one of the leather harnesses. What about her attracted him? After

Sheri Carson dumped him for Mike-the-muscleman his sophomore year in college, he'd rarely dated. Keeping his nose in a computer was safer than risking his heart and letting it crash like a hard drive infected with a nasty virus.

"C'mon, Uncle Evan. Aren't you going swimming?" His niece's dark brows lifted in challenge.

"Uh. . .shouldn't we find out where our tent is first?"

Taylor hoisted her backpack onto her shoulder and tucked her sleeping bag under one arm. She pointed toward the middle of the tents. "It's that one over there. Number five. We're sharing it with Alison Perry and her dad."

He followed his niece up a trail into a tent erected on top of a three-foot-high wooden platform. How was he supposed to share this single room with two teenage girls?

"Chill, Uncle Evan. Look." Taylor pointed toward the tent top. "There's a room divider we can unroll. I'll sleep on this side with Alison, and you and her dad can have that side."

Evan set his bag on one of the cots, feeling only marginally better. A thin cloth didn't seem like enough of a barrier between him and two noisy teens. How was he supposed to get any work done?

Outside, he heard a rooster crow and looked down at his tennis shoes to see if the crazy bird had left peck marks. He sure hoped they left that crazy attack-critter in its cage. He shook his head and let out a heavy breath. Was he ever out of his element!

The tent held four cots, and its sides were rolled up to let in the warm breeze. A gas lantern that sat on a small table separating the two beds on each side was the only source of light. Stairs leading out the back of the tent platform pulled him that direction. Behind and off to the left was a bathhouse and restroom facilities. The big man who captured the rooster walked behind the building, and a moment later, Evan heard the roar of a generator kick to life. Maybe they'd have warm water for showers—and a plug-in for his battery pack.

Mountains rose up in splendor behind the bathhouse. God sure had made this place beautiful. His gaze lifted to the sky, and he thought of how he'd skipped church the past two Sundays to work on his project. Guilt wormed its way through him, not for the first time. "Sorry, Lord. I promise to do better."

"What did you say?" Taylor peeked around the curtain and held it against her chin.

"Tay–lor!" Alison squealed, even though he hadn't so much as a glimpse of her.

"Nothing," he said.

"You'd better get ready if you're going swimming."

He shrugged. "I didn't bring a swimsuit. Didn't know I'd need one."

"Too bad." The curtain dropped back into place, and Taylor disappeared again. He heard her whisper something to her friend but couldn't make it out. Both girls giggled.

A short, thin man clomped up the front steps. He nodded and dropped his pack onto the empty cot. He held out his hand. "Charley Perry."

"Evan Parker."

The man's brows dipped. "Are you Taylor's father?"

Taylor snorted on the other side of the curtain—at least he thought it was her. Evan shook his head. "I'm her uncle."

"Nice to meet you. I was sitting in the front of your wagon, but you never looked up from your laptop."

"Sorry." Evan shrugged. "I'm on a tight deadline."

"Good luck with that up here. Don't know where you're going to find power for the next two weeks." He turned away and pulled some clothes and a flashy swimsuit from his duffel bag.

Evan wasn't ready to give up working on his project just yet, but things weren't looking too good. They weren't even a full day away from the ranch, and already they had no electricity.

He heard another generator fire up and walked to the front of the tent. Suddenly a thought sparked in his mind. Where there was a generator, there had to be power. All he needed now was a power strip.

❧

Bethany finished her walk around the perimeter of the camp, satisfied that everything looked in order. The scent of pine mixed with the fragrance of hamburgers cooking over an open flame on the grill her dad had made years ago.

Squeals and shouts of people at play echoed across the green valley. She stopped to watch the teens and their parents splashing in the cool water of the lake. If only she could recapture the joy of her youth, a time when worries and concerns didn't weigh her down.

"Here I go, ready or not." A husky boy took a running start and jumped off the end of the dock onto the colorful water blob. A skinny boy with lily-white skin flew high into the air, arms swirling, and landed in the lake with a splash. Bethany smiled, remembering the fun she'd had after they'd first installed the giant inflatable pillow.

Evan Parker's niece was next in line to jump on the blob. Taylor said something to the girl behind her and then ran hard, jumping into the air with a shrill squeal and onto the blob. The heavyset boy didn't go up into the air nearly as much as the skinny boy had, but his smile showed he still enjoyed the ride.

Behind the lake, the sun was already heading downward, its light soon to be blocked out by the tall mountains. She turned to leave and saw Mr. Parker tiptoeing his way, barefoot, over the rocky ground. His pants were rolled up, and Bethany sucked in her top lip to keep from grinning at his pale legs. She lifted her gaze to his as if drawn by an unknown source, and her heart skipped a beat at the vividness of his eyes. They were as blue as the sky, and at this elevation, the sky was even bluer than in the low country.

He spied her, waved, and jostled toward her, backpack in hand. "Hey, I was looking for you. Is there someplace I could charge the batteries for my laptop? I used up the juice on all three of the ones I brought with me."

Bethany resisted the urge to sigh and shake her head. The deadline the man said he was working toward must be really important for him to feel the need to use his vacation time. "I would imagine there's an outlet in the cookhouse that might be free."

"Great!"

She glanced down at his pale feet. "You really shouldn't be going barefoot. You might cut yourself on a rock."

He grinned, sending tingles dancing in her stomach. "I thought I might go walk around in the water."

"Don't say I didn't warn you." Without indicating for him to follow, she moseyed over to the canteen and cookhouse and entered through the back door. The sweet odor of cooling baked beans circulated around the smell of a freshly baked cake. Jenny Campbell, the trail cook, looked up from the bowl of coleslaw she was stirring and smiled.

"How's everything going, Jenny?" Bethany asked. Evan Parker padded in behind her.

"Good. The cake just needs to cool some, and then I can frost it. Everything else is ready if you want to ring the bell."

"Jim has a mess of burgers ready." Bethany glanced around the small kitchen and spied a power strip on the counter where the mixer and the light were still plugged in. She looked over her shoulder. "Looks like you're in luck."

Evan Parker must have spied the power strip, too, because his face lit up like a kid seeing his first Christmas tree. Bethany sucked in a breath at the difference it made. He was a handsome man when he wasn't scowling and his head wasn't buried in his laptop. His tan proved he spent time outdoors, even if his legs hadn't seen the light of day for a long while. Wide shoulders tapered down to a narrow waist. She forced herself to quit staring.

Jenny lifted both brows and gave her a knowing smile. Heat charged to Bethany's cheeks. She searched for something to do and grabbed the stack of Styrofoam plates and napkins and hurried toward the door.

"Um. . .you don't mind if I used your power strip for a while, do you, ma'am?" Evan's voice sounded behind her.

"No, I'm nearly done. All I'll need is a plug-in for the mixer."

"Great. Thanks. I'll just plug in my charger and get out of your way." He rustled through his pack, pulled out a charger with a battery attached, and plugged it into the strip. "I'll come back later and swap out the battery for another one."

Hugging the plates and napkins to her chest, Bethany waited at the door to make sure he didn't get in Jenny's way. Mealtimes observed a strict schedule.

He walked toward Bethany and grinned. "Thanks for allowing me to use your power."

She stepped outside, and he caught the screen door and closed it without letting it bang. She walked toward the picnic tables that sat between the tents and the lake, circling the campfire where Jim cooked the burgers.

"Can I carry that for you?" Evan glanced sideways at her.

She shook her head, pleased that he'd offered. "It's not heavy. If you're going in the water, you'd probably better do it now. We'll be eating soon, and the temperature will cool down fast once the sun sets."

"Yeah, I suppose I should check on Taylor." He looked toward the lake then back at her. "I can't imagine being able to enjoy such a view every day. Have you lived here long?"

"All my life. My great-grandparents bought the place and ran cattle. Not long after my dad took over the ranch, people started learning about the awesome beauty up here, and my parents decided to branch out. They started inviting city folks to visit."

"That must have been hard on you. To have to share your family and home with so many strangers." He stared at her, as if looking into her soul.

Bethany swallowed and broke the connection. As she'd grown older, she'd tried to be friendly and yet distance herself from their guests. As a teen, she'd longed for a close friend, but every time she got to know a girl and made a connection, her new friend would leave and go home. Maybe they'd write for a while, but usually by the time school started, the girls would quit contacting her. Losing a friend hurt more than not having one at all.

Most visitors talked about the view, the animals, or the ranch, but no man had ever considered how living in such an isolated place had affected her. His gaze was clear and curious.

"Sorry—didn't mean to venture into taboo territory." He shoved his hands into his pockets and stared at the lake.

"It's all right. I'm just not used to people asking me personal questions. Sharing the summers with others is all I can ever remember. I loved going on the trail rides as a kid and riding my horse."

"Do I sense a *but* coming?"

She shrugged one shoulder, not sure why she was confessing

to this stranger. "I guess I got tired of it as I grew older."

"Yeah, I've seen that with Taylor. She used to be happy playing board games or going to the park, but she seems to change every time I see her. She's not a little girl anymore, and I don't know this stranger who's inhabited her body."

Bethany peered sideways. Light brown stubble enhanced his jawline, making him look more manly. For some odd reason, she wanted to offer him encouragement. "It won't always be like that. Give her a few years, and she'll get her feet back on solid ground. I know I did."

He turned toward her and smiled. "Thanks. I needed to hear that."

"Maybe this time together will help your relationship with her."

Jim clanged the old-fashioned triangle, signaling that the burgers were ready. "Guess I'd better go help."

"Yeah, and I think I'd better get some shoes on before I cut my feet to shreds."

She smiled. "See you at dinner, tenderfoot."

His return grin warmed her as she hurried back to the kitchen for the pot of baked beans. Jenny was coming out the door with her arms filled with a huge bowl of coleslaw and bags of buns.

"Did you have a nice chat?" The cook waggled her brows.

Bethany rolled her eyes. "I was just being friendly to a guest."

"Uh-huh." Jenny pushed past her, chuckling.

Bethany grabbed the pot of beans and stood in the quiet of the small kitchen for a moment. Why was she attracted to Evan Parker? He was nothing like the few outgoing guys she'd dated in college. Outside, she set the beans on the serving table and went to pass out plates to help keep things moving quickly. Dripping teens lined up with their parents and took a plate and bun as fast as she could pass them out. They slathered on mayonnaise, ketchup, or mustard and then helped themselves to an array of garnishes.

"Mmm, sure smells good." One of the fathers smiled at Bethany and took a plate.

Three adolescents plopped down at the table nearest her and bit into their burgers. She liked to watch people's expressions as they tasted the homegrown beef for the first time. Her father prided himself on his quality cattle. But instead of eye-closing delight, all three faces scrunched up. The two boys leaned sideways and spat out their bites, while the girl swallowed hers then chased it with half a can of pop.

Bethany's heart lurched. What in the world could have caused such a reaction?

Glancing around at the others who'd gotten their burgers, she watched for their reactions. Every one was the same. Disgust. Revulsion.

She strode over to the table with the three teens, and they all stared wide-eyed at her. "What's wrong with the meat?"

The girl grabbed her can of root beer and took another drink. Bethany shifted her gaze to the biggest of the boys. He guzzled his drink and fanned his mouth. "It's too hot. Blazing hot."

"Yeah," the other boy said. "I guess we just aren't used to eating things as spicy as you guys out here do."

"They're not supposed to be hot at all. Not spicy hot, anyway. Let me see what I can find out."

She marched over to Big Jim, noticing more and more people were shoving aside their hamburgers. She didn't need this trouble.

"Stop serving the meat."

Both Jim and the next kids in line stared at her as if she'd gone crazy. She grabbed a plate and took a patty right off the grill. She sniffed it, savoring the beefy fragrance, then pinched off a small piece and put it in her mouth. Blazing fire ignited her senses and set her tongue burning. She leaned sideways and discreetly spit the half-chewed bite into her hand and dropped it on the ground. Her eyes watered, and she raced toward the drink table and grabbed a bottle of water. Her nose ran, and she sniffed as the fire in her mouth lessened.

Jim stomped his way toward her, the metal spatula still in his hand. "What's wrong?"

She held up her index finger and took another swig. "The meat is burning hot."

He shook his head. "Yeah, well, that's what happens when you take one right off the fire and cram it into your mouth."

"No, I mean it's loaded with hot sauce or cayenne pepper or something."

Jim's fuzzy gray brows dipped. "How is that possible?"

Bethany shook her head. "I don't know, but we have to do something fast. Look around you."

Not a soul was eating a burger, but they were scarfing down the baked beans and slaw.

"What do you want to do?" Jim crossed his arms over his massive chest.

"Can you run back to the ranch ASAP and have Polly fix up a bunch of sandwiches? The last thing we need is all these people leaving early and demanding a refund."

He nodded and marched back to the grill. "Folks," his deep voice boomed around the camp. "Let me have your attention. I apologize for the meat being so hot. Someone goofed somewhere. If you can hold out for a while longer, we'll have some sandwiches for you guys. There'll be a couple of cowboys singing 'round the fire in an hour. We hope you will join us."

Groans and grumbles sounded all around. Jim removed

the remaining half-cooked patties from the grill and dumped them back on the baking sheet with the rest of the raw burgers. He carried the pan to the kitchen then made a beeline for the Jeep. Bethany appreciated his making the announcement, although she should have done it. One round-faced boy piled his empty plate with sliced dill pickles and sat back down, while most of the people finished their side dishes. Some were leaving the tables and heading for their tents. It was best they shed their wet clothes before the temperature dropped, anyway.

Jenny hurried her way toward Bethany, her long brown braids bouncing on her chest and her eyes snapping. "I didn't do it. Just so you know. I never put hot sauce in the ground beef—at least not unless I'm making chili. Too many of the city folks can't tolerate it. I can't imagine what happened."

Bethany stared at the peaceful lake. The surface, no longer broken by rowdy kids, rippled gently from the light wind. "I don't understand how a mistake like this could have happened. Did Polly help with the meat this time?"

Jenny nodded. "Yes. Polly ground the meat in the ranch kitchen and shaped them into patties then stuck them in the freezer. I suppose she might have left the meat unattended at some point, since she sometimes had to help at the front desk when your dad was gone. I didn't even season it until we got here. Just added salt, pepper, and a little garlic. I'll go check the containers to make sure that I didn't get the wrong condiments in them somehow."

Bethany shook her head. It made no sense, but she had to get to the bottom of this. They needed this trip to be perfect so these folks would return someday and recommend Moose Valley Ranch to their friends. With the ranch's finances being stretched tight, they couldn't afford another mistake like this one.

four

"You girls quiet down over there."

Charley Perry's deep voice seemed out of place with his short stature, but Evan long ago learned not to judge a book by its cover. Giggles sounded from the far side of the curtain.

"You 'bout ready for lights-out?" Charley slipped on his flannel green plaid pajama shirt and tucked it into the bottoms. "Being out in the wilderness sure can wear a body out."

"I hear you." Evan grabbed his cell. "Just let me make one quick phone call, and then I'll be ready."

"Good luck with that. I tried earlier but couldn't get a signal up here." Charley yawned and scratched his belly then plopped down onto his cot.

Dressed in a long-sleeved gray pullover and comfortable navy sweatpants, Evan stood on the top step and flipped open his phone. The message SEARCHING FOR SERVICE shone on the screen. After a moment he lifted the phone higher in the air. "C'mon. C'mon."

The No SERVICE message flashed. "Great."

"What's so important that you've gotta call tonight?" Charley asked from inside the tent.

Evan flipped the phone shut and then opened it again. Still no luck. "I'm working on a project and need to make regular reports. Too bad they don't have Internet service here, or I could just e-mail them. I think I'll try getting away from the tent."

He slipped on his socks and shoes. Using his phone for a flashlight, he followed the path to the picnic tables. When the light on the display screen dimmed, he snapped the phone shut and climbed onto one of the picnic tables. He tried again, and this time when the ROAMING sign came on, he punched in the project manager's number. The phone was quiet for a moment; then he got a busy signal. He looked at the screen and realized the call had disconnected.

Sighing, he closed the phone and shoved it into his pocket. The picnic table creaked under his weight. A short distance away, soft lights flickered behind the canvas walls of the tents, reminding him of the ceramic Christmas village his sister set up every holiday season. Pine trees rose up black against the sky, illuminated by the moon just rising. He lifted his face to the sky and sucked in a breath at the myriad stars shining like diamonds against black velvet. "You sure made some majestic places, Lord."

He felt torn between wanting to spend this time with Taylor and being faithful to the company that contracted him as a video game developer. Trying to do both wasn't working too well. After dinner he'd worked another hour and a half outside the cook shed while he still had daylight. The singing cowboys around the campfire and the dirty looks Taylor cast his way had finally pulled him from his work.

Evan heaved a sigh. He didn't like disappointing family. Maybe he should forget his work and try harder to join in the activities. He'd just have to put in extra hours when he got home to make up for it. With his eyes on the sky, he spent the next few minutes in prayer. Somehow he needed to find some answers.

Evan yawned and started to jump off the picnic table, but a noise halted his steps. Big Jim had warned them all about venturing away from the group during the day or straying from camp at night. Bears inhabited the area, as well as mountain lions, but Evan never thought they'd stray into the camp with so many people around. His heart pounded. Could he outrun a bear to his tent? But then what good would a bit of canvas do in deterring a determined beast—and he couldn't very well lead it straight to his niece. Swallowing hard, he strained to hear the creature again.

Soft whispers and giggles sounded to his right, and he spun around. The table creaked again beneath his weight.

"What was that?" a shaky female voice called out.

"I don't know. Maybe this wasn't a good idea."

Evan recognized the male voice as belonging to one of the boys who rode in his wagon. So, he'd interrupted a little romantic tryst. He couldn't help grinning as his heart slowed back to a normal pace. After so long outside, Evan's eyes had become accustomed to the dark, but he barely made out the shape of a boy and girl standing a dozen feet away. He considered growling and sending the kids screaming back to their tents, but that would be too mean.

"Shh. I heard something again," the girl whispered.

Evan bounced on the table, making it squeak. The girl let out a yelp and took off running with the boy close on her heels. He chuckled and stepped down to the bench seat and onto the ground. Nope, no bear this time, but as he neared his tent, he couldn't help thinking again how that flimsy canvas wouldn't keep out a determined bear if it wanted in.

❧

The morning sun erupted over the eastern ridge in brilliant glory, bringing with it the promise of clear skies and warmer temperatures. Bethany stretched and made her way to the cookhouse. Today would be a good one. She could feel it.

Ed had been crowing off and on for a good hour, and Bethany couldn't help remembering how the old bird had attacked Evan Parker's shoes. She smiled at the mental picture of the prancing man trying to get away. She shook her head. "Shame on me for taking pleasure in someone else's distress."

She'd been raised a Christian and had attended church until age twelve, when her mother died, but after that her father had rarely taken her. He missed his wife and buried his sorrows in work. She thought of the small community church she sometimes attended in Denver. The people were friendly enough, but she hadn't been able to find what she needed to fill the emptiness inside her. She stared at the trio of peaks glistening in the morning light. Why was it she felt closer to God when she was outside and away from town and church?

The door to the cookhouse squeaked as she pulled it open. Jenny, always an early riser, was hard at work browning a mess of bacon and sausage. The scent of the meat and biscuits baking filled the room and made Bethany's stomach grumble. She snitched a slice of cooked bacon. "How are things going? What can I do to help?"

"Fine, and you can fill that other baking sheet with biscuits. The ones in the oven are about done."

Bethany did as ordered. She might be the boss's daughter, but out here each person had a job she or he was responsible for, and she didn't mind helping the others. They'd help her if she needed it.

"Are the city slickers stirring yet?" Jenny tucked her spatula under several rows of bacon and laid them in a serving pan layered on the bottom with paper towels.

"Some. They've hardly done anything and are already tuckered out."

"Must be the fresh mountain air getting to them." The women shared a chuckle.

Bethany removed the golden biscuits from the oven and placed them on the counter then slid the uncooked batch in. She stacked the hot biscuits in a large, rectangular pan and set it on the warming tray.

"Just wait until next week. I'll have to serve breakfast a whole hour later because they'll be so pooped out." Jenny chuckled, and Bethany shook her head. It was an ongoing joke, though the cook always stuck rigidly to the meal schedule.

Jenny shoveled the remaining sausage links into the stainless steel serving dish then dumped the bacon at the other end of the rectangular pan and set it in the warming tray. "I just need to pour the gravy into the serving pan and scramble another batch of eggs. You want to ring the bell?"

"Sure. Everything looks great. Can't wait to eat." Bethany went outside the cookhouse and unlatched the upper half of the wooden wall on one side of the building. With the wall down, their guests could walk right up to the buffet and serve themselves. She tugged a stack of plates closer to the edge so they'd be within easy reach and then checked the silverware and napkins.

"I guess you're eager to see that good-looking greenhorn again." Jenny glanced up from her cooking eggs and sent Bethany a teasing glance.

Evan Parker invaded her mind, and her heart flip-flopped. She glanced over to where his batteries were still charging then peeked back at the cook. "Which greenhorn are you referring to? There are several nice-looking men on this trip."

Jenny grinned, her eyes sparkling. "Did I say it was a man?"

Bethany opened her mouth to respond then closed it. "Uh. . .no, I just assumed that's what you meant."

"Well. . .for the record, he is cute, even if he is a bit technically minded."

Bethany resisted commenting because it would only stir up Jenny to teasing her more. How had the cook noticed her interest in the computer geek? Other than when he first came to the cookhouse to ask about charging his batteries, she and Evan Parker hadn't been together where Jenny might have seen them. She scratched her head and walked outside where she picked up the metal striker and ran it around the inside of the triangle. The strong, clear ring brought the few folks sitting around the remains of last night's campfire to their feet. Others scurried out of their tents and down the steps. Bethany couldn't help searching for Evan Parker. Would he be at breakfast? Or had he stayed up late last night working on his project?

She hooked the striker to the bottom of the triangle and went back inside the cookhouse. The man wasn't her type at all. She preferred tall cowboys with dark eyes and dark hair, like her father had been when he was younger. Okay, Evan Parker was tall, she'd give him that—and had shoulders wide enough to lean on and blue eyes to die for. Gritting her teeth, she shoved thoughts of the computer geek aside. They had nothing in common, so why did he keep straying into her thoughts?

She poured a pot of coffee into the large carafe and started another pot brewing. With everything in order, she filled a plate and sat down at the small table to eat with Jenny while the guests filled their plates. They were close enough if anyone needed help.

The salty bacon teased her tongue and crunched in her teeth. A swig of coffee filled her stomach with its soothing warmth. Murmurs of conversation battled the clank of the big serving spoons and tongs as the guests helped themselves to the array of food.

"Are things ready for lunch?" Bethany held her mug with both hands and peered over the top at Jenny.

The cook nodded. "I've got fixings for sandwiches and am making a pot of chicken noodle soup to go with it. I'll clean up here and cook the soup then meet you at the lunch site by noon."

Bethany nodded, grateful that her father had the wisdom to keep Jenny on staff. The woman had cooked for them for the last five summers. With her kids grown and her husband deceased, the job gave her something to do, as well as a much-needed income.

They ate in companionable silence for a few minutes; then Big Jim banged through the back door, filling the whole entryway. A muscle in his jaw ticked, and he stared at her with narrowed eyes.

Bethany's heart sank down to her belly. "What's wrong?"

He glanced at the line of guests at the buffet and motioned his head toward the door. "Got something to show you."

Thankfully, she'd just finished her breakfast. She had a feeling the news he had to share would have affected her appetite. Big Jim was normally lively and jovial, but not this morning. He didn't even take time to grab a cup of coffee.

Outside and away from the guests, she turned to him. "Tell me straight. What is it?"

"Better that I show you." He strode toward the wagons, and she searched the area for signs of trouble. Occasionally, some critter wandered into a tent when a guest had left food exposed, but that rarely happened with so many people around.

Jim strode around the back of the last wagon and pointed to the wheel. Bethany pursed her lips. A flat tire. Well, it wasn't the end of the world or the first time a tire had gone down. "What's the big deal? Just air it back up."

Jim gave her an exasperated shake of his head like a father might give a troublesome child. He gently grasped her upper arm and propelled her forward. He stopped beside the next wagon, and her eyes drifted downward. This wagon had not one but two flat tires.

Her gaze flew up to his. "This can't be an accident. One tire, maybe, but not three."

"Oh, it's not just three. The back tires on the Jeep are flat, too."

"Why would someone do this?" Evan Parker leaped into her mind again. Surely he wouldn't do something like this just so he could stay near a power source. No, he didn't seem the kind of man to play pranks, but what did she really know about him? "Maybe some of the teens couldn't sleep last night and got bored."

Jim shrugged one big shoulder. "Maybe, but I can't help feeling there's more to this than meets the eye."

"I'll air up the Jeep tires and then start on the wagons," Bethany said. "You go on and get some breakfast."

"You sure? I don't mind doing it."

She smiled and nodded. "Go on. This won't take too long, and let's try to keep it quiet and not let the guests know there's been trouble."

"Good idea. If it is some of the teens, maybe we can catch them if they don't know that we're on to them." He turned and strode toward the cookhouse.

Bethany opened the back of the Jeep and found the long hose that hooked to the small air compressor they always brought along. A hiss of air escaped as she attached the other end to the Jeep's right rear tire. She turned on the rumbling compressor and started the air pumping.

She looked back toward camp to see if anyone was watching her. If one of them had done this, surely they'd want to see the reaction of whoever discovered their deed. But nobody seemed to be paying the least bit of attention to her.

Thank goodness they hadn't damaged the tires. If they'd been slashed, the whole trip would have come to a quick halt until replacement tires could be provided.

First, the too-spicy food, and now this. Was someone deliberately trying to mess up this trip? Or was it just some strange, unfortunate coincidence?

five

Bethany rubbed lotion on her hands and worked the soothing cream into her cracked fingertips. Washing dishes for fifty people did a number on her hands. She stood at the door of her tent and scanned the crowded campsite. Teens and their chaperones sat listening to Steve spin a yarn about the olden days while two other cowboys played a banjo and a harmonica.

The sun had already set on the second day of their tour, but the sky was still a dark blue and hadn't yielded to the blackness of night that would soon surround them. Bethany longed for some quiet and grabbed her rifle. With all the noise in the camp, it wasn't likely a wild animal would venture close, but she would be prepared if it did.

She zipped her tent shut and then her jacket and strode past the rows of tents. Lantern lights flickered behind a few of the canvas sides, but most people were still down at the camp, making s'mores and enjoying Steve's tale about a lost gold shipment. The ground crunched beneath her boots, and she angled over toward the horses. Under lantern light, Big Jim was brushing down a bay mare, one of the dozen head they kept on hand for horseback riding.

"How's it going?"

Jim turned her direction, but his face was blotted out by the growing darkness. The light shone behind him, outlining his silhouette. "All right. The horses weathered today's trail rides okay, even though a few of the kids ran them more than they should have."

"Kids like to gallop, that's for sure." A gray gelding nickered at Bethany and stuck his long head over the fence, looking for a handout. She patted his forehead then smoothed down his forelock, remembering with a smile how one girl had called them bangs. "Sorry, boy, I don't have any treats for you."

"There's something I've been meaning to tell you ever since breakfast." Jim patted the mare he'd been brushing and turned her loose in the corral. He rolled up the lead rope and stared at Bethany. With his left side facing the lantern, she saw a muscle tick in his jaw. He studied the ground then looked up. "It wasn't any of these kids that let the air out of the tires."

Bethany sucked in a breath. "Then who was it?"

Jim shrugged. "I don't know for sure, but I found a set of hoof prints close to the wagons."

She huffed out a half laugh and relaxed her shoulders. "The horses have been all over this area. What's so unusual about that?"

"I found where the horse had been tied up. There were quite a few prints there, all belonging to the same animal and someone wearing boots. The horse was wearin' egg bar shoes, and you know we don't use those on our horses."

"Isn't that a shoe that is shaped like an oval and has a bar across the back?"

Jim nodded and leaned his arms over the top rail of the corral. "I'll make some calls and see which ranchers around here use egg bars. Whoever let out the air rode a long ways to play a prank."

Bethany lifted her boot to the bottom rail and set her rifle against the gate post. "But who? And why?"

"I don't know. But I think we should be extra watchful on this trip."

"Yeah. I agree." She thought of their neighbors and the

people in town, but not one person stood out who might want to cause them trouble. People in the high country generally stuck together and helped each other. "Well, I'm going for a walk before it's totally dark. I'll keep my ears open."

"It's already dark. Want some company?"

She smiled. "Thanks, but I need some time alone. These teenagers make too much noise."

A loud laugh from the edge of camp sounded, followed by a girl's squeal.

"I hear ya." He took the lantern and headed back toward the campfire.

Bethany pushed away from the corral and picked up her rifle. The tire incident couldn't have been by chance. They were miles away from anyone else, so someone would have had to deliberately seek them out. Someone who knew their schedule. A shiver raced down her back.

She walked along the path the horses used during the trail rides. She knew this area by heart and didn't need a light to guide her. The music and chatter of the guests faded, and the sounds of nature soothed her with their serenade.

She topped a hill and walked down the other side, effectively blocking out the glow of the campfire. A strange light flickered ahead in the navy twilight. Bethany slid to a halt. What in the world? It fluttered around like a giant firefly; then it faded and disappeared. Her heart stampeded, and she lifted the rifle. The light reappeared, closer than before. She took a step backward.

Scuffling footsteps drew nearer. The light dimmed again, disappeared, and then shone bright once more. Her breath grew ragged, and she clutched the weapon tighter.

The blue glow looked unnatural in the wilderness setting. Suddenly, she heard whistling. A tune that pulled her back to church. One of the worship songs she'd learned as a kid.

The footsteps stopped about fifty feet in front of her. The light dipped down and moved around about a foot off the ground. Bethany's limbs grew weak with relief as she realized what she'd been seeing. A cell phone.

"Are you lost?" she called out, glad the darkness covered the red on her cheeks.

The light jerked, and whoever it was must have straightened. The phone stayed black, and the person didn't answer for a few moments. "Uh. . .a man never likes to admit such a thing to a lady."

Her heart constricted. She recognized that voice. "Mr. Parker?"

"Busted."

"What are you doing out here?"

A cool breeze whipped her hair into her face. She brushed it back and looped it over her ear. Laughter drifted her way, and she strained to hear where it was coming from. Definitely not camp.

"I was climbing trees."

"What?"

"Trees. You know. Climbing." He flipped open the phone, illuminating his face in the stark darkness.

"You're serious."

He nodded.

"Why?"

He shrugged and looked to his right. "I. . .uh. . .was trying to get up high enough to get phone service."

Bethany shook her head. "That's crazy. You could have gotten hurt. And you're not supposed to leave camp alone, especially at night. Did anyone even know where you were?"

"No, not really." The light faded, and he left it off. "I'm not exactly used to reporting in to my fourteen-year-old niece."

Having an argument in the dark was weird, but she wasn't about to ask him to turn on the light. So much for time alone. "We have rules for a reason, Mr. Parker."

"Call me Evan."

"Woo-hoo! That's what I'm talking about." A loud voice carried across the quiet landscape, and a fire flamed to life in the distance.

What now?

She reached out and grabbed Evan's arm, tugging him up the hill. "Come with me."

"Who's out there?" he asked.

"I don't know, but I'm going to find out." As they topped the hill, the soft glow of the campfire illuminated the horizon. She released her hold on him. "There's camp. You can make it fine from here."

"You're not going out there alone."

"I'm not alone. I have my rifle."

He snorted a laugh. "I'm going with you."

"No."

"Yes."

She walked toward his voice. "You're a guest. I do this for a living. Go back to camp."

He didn't say anything, but his warm breath fanned her face. Given another day and time, she might have enjoyed a walk at night with the handsome man. She shook her head and stomped down the hill. What had gotten into her?

Dreaming of walking in the dark with a man who climbed trees in hopes of making his cell phone work. Oh brother. She missed the comforts of the city, too, but this guy was really out there. Her pace slowed as she neared the small campfire. Illuminated by the fire, a lanky boy from the junior high group passed a bottle to another teen.

"Whoo-wee, that stuff sure has a kick."

"Hey, give it back. I only got a little swig."

Bethany ground her teeth together. She ought to go get Jim, but then she ought to be able to handle two kids on her own. She hoisted her rifle and marched into camp. Maybe she could scare some sense into them. "Just what do you think you're doing?"

On the far side of the campfire, the tallest youth spun around looking startled, and then a cocky smirk lifted one side of his mouth. The shorter boy stuck a bottle behind his back.

"We're just havin' some fun. Come and join us, why don't you?" The tall boy ran his hand through his hair. "My name's Donny. Aren't you Miss Schaffer?"

Bethany ignored his unskilled attempt to flirt and lowered her rifle. The boys may have broken several rules by taking off alone, starting a fire, and drinking liquor, but she certainly wasn't going to shoot one of them. The campfire popped and flickered, stretching its fingers of light into the night, illuminating the teenagers and casting spooky shadows in her direction.

"It's dangerous to be out here alone, especially after dark, and this is a family camp. Liquor isn't allowed."

Donny hooked his thumbs in his front pockets and swaggered toward her like a cowpoke. If she hadn't been angered by the tomfoolery, she might have laughed. Did the youth actually think she'd be impressed?

"Put out that fire, and let's get back to camp. You two are in a world of trouble."

The shorter boy kicked a little dirt onto the fire but not enough to snuff out the flame. Donny smiled, reminding her of the serpent that tempted Eve in the Garden of Eden. "Why don't you just sit down and have a drink with us? Nobody would have to know."

"Don't be ridiculous. Kill the fire, and let's go." Bethany's heartbeat galloped. This kid didn't look as if he'd go easy. She heard a twig snap to her right and glanced into the inky blackness.

Donny yanked the rifle from her hand, jerking her gaze back to him. "C'mere, Fred."

The boy by the fire hesitated. Donny glared over his shoulder, putting Fred's feet into action. Bethany swallowed the lump in her throat and took a step backward.

"Oh no you don't." Donny grabbed her wrist.

A shiver charged down her spine. She could get away easily if she ran into the darkness, but she wouldn't leave her rifle with this delinquent and possibly put others in harm's way. Fred, almost as wide as he was tall, with pimples all over his face, stopped beside his friend. Donny held out the rifle, and Fred looked at it as if it were poison.

"Hold this for a minute."

When Fred didn't respond, Donny shoved the rifle at the boy. If she could distract Donny, maybe she could snatch the Winchester from Fred and run for help. Big Jim would come looking anyway if she didn't return soon—unless he was too busy working to notice. Or maybe she could fire the rifle into the air. That would bring Jim fast.

She tried to wrench her arm free, but Donny was stronger than he looked. A good five inches taller than she, he was lean and solid where Fred was wide and dumpy. He tightened his grip and forced her closer then grabbed her other arm.

Her pulse skyrocketed. "Let me go, boy. So far you've just broken the rules, but now you're bordering on assault."

"Aw, don't you want to have some fun?" He pulled her against his chest, and the stench of the liquor on his breath forced her to turn her head.

She shoved against his torso. "Let me go."

"Yeah, Donny. Turn her loose."

"Shut up, Fred." He lowered his face to hers. "You're a hottie with all that golden hair sparkling in the firelight."

She spun her face away, and his moist lips slid across her cheek. One hand raced around her back, anchoring her body against his, and he used his other hand to force her face back toward his.

She wasn't about to give him what he wanted. She lifted her foot behind her and slammed it into his shin. He cursed and hopped on one foot but didn't release her. He called her a foul name and grabbed her hair. "You'll pay for that."

She heard the scrabble of hurrying footsteps and saw a man step into the light of the campfire. Hope emboldened her. Donny was still hissing from pain and didn't notice the man.

"Turn me loose, kid, or you're going to be sorry."

"Ooh, you're scaring me." He chuckled and angled his face downward again. "Like you said, it's dangerous to be out here all alone."

"She's not alone."

Donny froze. Slowly he lifted his head and released her. Bethany scrambled away and looked for Fred. He sat by the fire with his head in his hands. Suddenly, Donny spun around, his fist colliding with Evan Parker's jaw. Evan stumbled backward but regained his balance and held up the rifle he'd somehow taken from Fred. Donny halted and glared at the man. The boy's hands lifted slowly into the air.

"You okay?" Evan glanced at her.

"Yeah." She tried to calm her trembling hands. "But let me have the rifle. How about you?"

His smile warmed her insides and calmed the jagged edges of her nerves. "I'm fine."

She reclaimed her Winchester. That had been a close call. She didn't want to think how far Donny might have gone.

Evan grabbed Donny by the arm. The fight must have gone out of the boy, because he just stood there looking at the ground.

She glanced at the campfire. "Let's take them to base camp; then I'll come back and deal with this fire. It looks contained for the moment."

"Come on, we're heading back." Evan looked at Fred.

The boy lumbered to his feet, looking repentant. He shuffled toward them. "Nobody was s'posed to get hurt. We just wanted to have some fun."

Bethany thought of the archery lessons, swimming, and horseback riding that had been offered that day. She knew they couldn't please everyone who came to the ranch, but they tried hard, and it bothered her that this boy had been dissatisfied.

They escorted the boys back to camp and found two relieved fathers.

"I was just heading out to search for them—and you." Jim gave her a scolding glare.

"I'd have been back sooner, but I ran into trouble." She told them what happened, getting stern looks from Donny's father. "I'm sorry, but you'll have to leave the tour. The boys knew the rules and willingly broke them our second day out. If Mr. Parker hadn't happened along when he did, these boys could be facing charges for something worse than assaulting him and me. Jim can drive you back to the ranch in the morning, and my father will have our attorney contact you."

Four sets of worried eyes stared back. "Surely we could work out something without getting the authorities involved," Donny's father said.

Bethany shrugged. "You need to realize the seriousness of what your son did. I'll let my father decide what to do, but you'll be leaving come morning."

As everyone drifted away, Evan gently rested his hand on

her shoulder. She flinched but didn't move. "Are you sure you're all right?"

She looked up, surprised to see one side of his jaw swelling. "We need to get some ice on that."

He wriggled his jaw then grimaced. "Guess he got me better than I realized."

In the cookhouse, she flipped on the light. The flickering bulb that normally didn't throw out enough light looked bright after the darkness of the night. The generator hummed just outside, but the cookhouse seemed unusually quiet without Jenny bustling about. Bethany opened the freezer and grabbed two ice cubes then put them in a plastic sandwich bag and sealed it shut. She placed the ice inside a dishrag and handed it to Evan.

"You'll probably be a little sore in the morning. Does it hurt much?"

He shrugged one shoulder and held the pack against his cheek. "My jaw's a little sore and my head aches, but it's nothing I can't live with." In spite of everything that had happened, a smile lingered in his azure eyes.

Bethany pulled out a chair. "Have a seat. I'll get you some aspirin. Would you like some coffee? I could make some."

He glanced at the refrigerator. "I could really use a pop. I prefer my caffeine cold."

"Pop it is." She snagged two cans, got a couple of aspirin from the medicine box, and sat down across the table from him. She popped the lid of one can and slid it and the pills toward him.

"Thanks." He threw the pills into his mouth and swigged down half the can of pop. "Mmm, that tastes good. I have to admit, I've been having caffeine withdrawal."

She smirked. "I don't see how. I've noticed that you're usually first in line when the snack bar opens."

His shy smile sent pleasing tingles racing through her.

"Don't let those two bad apples spoil your trip, okay?"

Bethany blinked and opened her mouth, but nothing came out. He took a hit for her and had the bruises to prove it, yet he was concerned for *her*? She stared into his eyes, unable to look away. "How can you be so upbeat after what just happened?"

He cautiously opened his mouth, worked his jaw sideways, and pressed the ice pack against it again. "Just a God thing, I guess. God's grace is sufficient for any situation."

"If you hadn't wanted to use your phone so badly, you wouldn't have been out there to help me."

"Bingo! God put me there because He was watching out for you and knew you'd need help. He sees our needs even before we're aware of them."

He stared into her eyes, as if begging her to believe him. Her mouth suddenly dry, she broke her gaze and downed a third of her pop, then set the can down. "I'd better call my dad and let him know what happened."

She walked over to the satellite phone that was plugged into the charger right beside Evan's computer battery. Behind her, his chair scooted across the floor.

"You have a sat phone?"

She couldn't help smiling at the reverence in his voice.

"Yeah, it's necessary in case of an emergency." She lifted it from the charger and turned to face him. "Would you like to use it when I'm done?"

A wide grin tugged at his lips, and he nodded. His stunning smile made her legs go weak. If she didn't watch herself, she was going to be in for a world of hurt when Evan Parker returned home.

six

Bethany sat down on a log bench that overlooked a scenic view of the mountains. She sipped her coffee and watched the drifting clouds. One looked like a dolphin and another like a long-faced man with a hooked nose and open mouth. Her mother had played the game with her when she was young. Bethany sighed.

How many weeks had passed since she'd thought of her mama? She no longer endured the stabbing pain she'd once felt but could now cherish the memories. Most girls seemed closer to their dads, but she had always had a special bond with her mother.

Maybe it had something to do with the fact that her mom homeschooled her. Or maybe because they went to church together. She'd never considered that before.

Evan Parker's words once again lingered in her mind. *"God put me there because He was watching out for you and knew you'd need help. He sees our needs even before we're aware of them."*

Could that really be true?

But how? If God saw their needs, then why were they in such a financial bind? Why did He take her mother away when Bethany loved and needed her so much?

Bethany wanted to believe—to grasp the peace she'd had as a child, but it was so hard. Still, there was something awesomely appealing about the almighty God seeing and anticipating her desires. Is that why Evan was on this tour? Because she needed him?

She snorted a laugh and shook her head. The last thing

she needed was a geeky city boy who couldn't leave his toys behind long enough to take a vacation with his niece.

An eagle screeched and drifted high above her, pulling her gaze upward. She watched as it lowered, wings spread wide, and glided to a stop. From this distance she couldn't tell if it had a nest on the craggy mountain ridge, but eagles had always fascinated her.

Girlish squeals sounded behind her, and she stood. Time to get to work. With Jim gone to take the two boys and their dads back to the lodge, she had extra chores. They'd have to spend another day at this camp since they couldn't leave until Jim returned. Trail rides were scheduled next, and horses needed to be saddled.

She returned her cup to the kitchen and made sure Jenny had the breakfast cleanup under control, then headed toward the corral. Evan's words returned to taunt her mind. If God was watching out for her, that meant He still cared about her. Her stomach twisted. He'd never left. She was the one who'd gotten angry after her mother's death. She was the one who'd walked away from Him. But how could she find her way back after so long?

She shook her head and smiled at some teens singing and doing a silly dance around the campfire. Most of the kids who visited Moose Valley were great kids just out for an adventure. From time to time, they'd get the troublemakers like the pair who'd been drinking.

Glancing at her watch, she noted the time. Almost nine o'clock. She'd take the riders on a different trail that would make the rides longer and kill more time today. Since they weren't supposed to be in this camp again today, she hadn't planned activities, but she could always wing it.

Footsteps sounded behind her, and she turned. Evan jogged toward her, the sun gleaming off his brown hair. Her heart flip-flopped and her limbs suddenly felt weak. His megawatt smile revealed straight, white teeth, and his injured jaw looked puffy and purple in the daylight. He was looking less and less like a nerd to her and more and more like a man she'd like to get to know. But what for? He'd be leaving soon.

Her smile slipped, and he slid to a halt. His grin dimmed in response to hers. "Hey, I uh. . .just wanted to say thanks again for letting me use the sat phone. I let my boss know that I'm out in the boonies and can't get reception on my cell. He said not to worry about checking in until I get back to civilization."

For some odd reason, her heart sank. She didn't like how he referred to her home. His attitude just proved that there was no reason to lower her guard.

"No problem. Are you going riding today?"

He walked beside her and stared ahead at the corral. She glanced at him, and he looked as if his jaw was set. Must not hurt him too badly if he could clench it.

"You're not afraid of horses, are you?"

His gaze darted sideways, and she grinned.

"You are!"

"No, not exactly scared of them. But they *are* the biggest animals I've ever encountered."

Bethany shook her head. "Most of these trail horses are just big babies. They want snacks and to be cared for like any other pet. Not that they are pets."

"I don't even have a dog."

"Do you have a roommate?" Bethany opened the door to the tack shed that held all the riding equipment.

"No, I live by myself."

She looped three bridles over one arm and handed another three to him. "You've been drafted to be my assistant since Jim's still gone."

His vivid eyes widened, but he reached out and took the bridles. "I have no idea what to do with this—other than to use it to steer the horse."

"Well, city boy, looks like you're going to learn."

She opened the corral gate and whistled. Evan came in behind her and closed the gate. Bethany suddenly stopped. Her heart jolted, and she counted the horses. "What in the world?"

"What's wrong?"

"Half of the horses are gone." She paced the wide corral, checking the railing for breaks, with Evan close on her heels.

He glanced back toward the cookhouse. "Could some of the teens have taken them?"

"I hadn't thought of that." She marched toward the tack shed and looked inside. Enough light shone through the door to illuminate the small room. "All of the saddles and bridles are still here, so it's not likely any kids are out riding."

She closed the door, thankful that at least none of their equipment had been stolen, but then saddles and bridles were cheap compared to horses.

"So, what do you think happened?" Evan asked. "How could they have gotten out if the gate was shut?"

"That's what I'm trying to figure out. The rails look fine." She stopped and faced him. He was a guest and shouldn't even know about their problems, but she needed an ally. "They couldn't have gotten out unless someone released them on purpose."

He shoved his hands into his pockets. His saddle-brown hair jutted up in cute spikes, reminding her of a porcupine. "Why would anyone release some of the horses and not all of them?"

She pressed her lips together and considered how much to tell him. Normally, she never got this friendly with a guest, but he'd come to her rescue, and for some reason, she wanted to tell him. "I think someone has been sabotaging this trip. First, the food was tampered with, then someone let air out of several tires on the wagons and Jeep the first night we were here. Now the missing horses. Too many problems to be a coincidence."

"Hmm." He placed his index finger over his lips and tapped them. Then he ran his hand over his swollen, purple jaw and winced. His hand dropped to his side. "You may be right, but why would someone want to cause you problems? Do you have any enemies?"

"No. None that I know of. I can't imagine who could be doing this." Bethany lifted a bridle off her arm and trapped a black gelding against the rails. She slipped the bit into his mouth and slid the headpiece over his ears, then hooked the throat latch. "I'll take this horse and see if I can find the others. I don't want the other guests to get wind that there are problems." She looked down at the ground. "I shouldn't even have told you."

He stood there for a moment with his face pointed at the sky. Had she offended him? Was he praying?

He rubbed the back of his neck and looked deep in thought. Bethany remembered what his niece had said about him needing time to process his thoughts. She led the gelding over near the gate and tied the reins to the railing. If she were lucky, she could find the horses and bring them back quickly. She'd have to get Steve to start another archery session to distract the guests—or maybe a fishing contest, and by the time they were finished, she should have all the horses back and saddled.

A sudden thought buzzed in her mind. "You know, the horses must have been released in the past few hours, or else Jim would have noticed them missing when he fed them earlier."

"We could question the campers and see if anyone would confess."

Bethany shook her head. "Teens aren't the best at admitting their faults. I doubt that would work unless someone saw the horses being released."

"You want me to ask around?"

"No. Let me go see if I can find them first." Patting the gelding, she stared at the camp. She had hoped her problems would disappear with the two troublemaking boys Jim took back first thing this morning. These guests would never want to return if they knew all that had happened.

Evan went back to watching the sky. Suddenly he snapped his fingers and strode toward her, still carrying the bridles. "I have an idea."

She ran her hand over the gelding's rump and met Evan in the middle of the corral. "What idea?"

"What if we make the campers think that the horses gone missing was planned? We could pretend rustlers stole them and let the campers hike out in groups to find them. Maybe even offer some kind of reward to the winners."

She shook her head at the crazy suggestion, but even as she did, she saw the beauty of his plan. It could work. The three wagon drivers, Steve, Benny, and herself, could each head up a group and make sure none of the greenhorns got hurt. It could actually be fun. A smile worked its way to her lips, and she refrained from reaching out and hugging the man who'd just solved her dilemma. He was a pleasant surprise, and she enjoyed his quiet company. Now they were partners in crime—sort of. "I like it. Let's do it."

&

"I bet the horses are over this hill." Taylor raced Alison, Misty, and Sarah James to the top of the hill.

"Yeah, we'll be the winners for sure." Sarah heaved a breath, and her short, stubby legs pumped as she tried to keep up with the taller, leaner girls.

Evan walked with several other chaperones and parents, following at a much more relaxed pace. He didn't want to admit it, but the altitude must be getting to him. Though he jogged regularly, this morning's walk had left him winded and feeling more tired than it should have. He scratched his arm and massaged his achy forehead.

Knee-high grass swished as they plowed through it. Wildflowers in yellow, white, and purple dotted the area, and with the mountains ahead, it was a scene worthy of a painter's canvas. He lifted his digital camera and snapped a picture. If only he could capture such a scene in his video games, but that was the job of the graphic artist, not the computer engineer.

Mrs. James jogged up beside him, breathing hard, and Evan resisted rolling his eyes. It seemed like every time he stepped outside, she managed to worm her way up next to him. "This is quite an adventure, isn't it, Mr. Parker? Just imagine. . .rustlers. Why it's enough to make a woman faint."

He glanced sideways at the slightly overweight brunette, hoping that she wasn't serious. He'd be more than winded if he had to help carry her back to camp. She wasn't a bad-looking woman, but he wasn't interested. A honey-blond with brown eyes so dark he could barely make out the pupils lingered in his mind. He'd hoped that he and Taylor could have been in the group Bethany Schaffer led, but at the last minute, Taylor decided she wanted to go with Alison's group, and he couldn't very well go in a different one than his niece.

The balmy sunshine warmed him, and the high altitude made catching his breath more difficult after the vigorous walk. A nagging pain stabbed his head. He swiped at a trickle of sweat, rolled up his shirtsleeves, and scratched at a red spot on his arm. Must be a bug bite. The difference in the nighttime and daytime temperatures amazed him. Short-sleeve weather by day, but he needed a jacket after the sun set, taking the day's heat with it.

"What kind of work do you do, Mr. Parker?" Mrs. James fanned her face with her hand and blinked her gray eyes at him like a schoolgirl. Her cheeks were bright red, but he didn't know if it was from exertion or a blush.

"I'm a computer engineer. I've been an instructor at the University of Wyoming, but now—"

High-pitched shrieks pulled his attention to the top of the hill. Ahead of them, four girls squealed and bounced up and down.

"There they are!"

"I see three of them."

Taylor looked over her shoulder and seemed to scan the group. Her eyes locked with his, and she actually smiled at him. Evan's heart tightened. He smiled and waved back.

Benny, the young man on horseback who was leading the group, rode up the hill and reined to a stop. The girls looked up at the handsome young man, as if seeking his approval.

"Those girls sure do have an eye for that hot ranch hand," Mrs. James said.

Evan scowled. "Yeah, I noticed." Benny may not be near Evan's age, but he was far too mature for a fourteen-year-old. Still, he had to give the man credit. He'd never once encouraged the girls' attention whenever Evan had seen him out among them.

Benny spoke something into his satellite phone and turned his horse toward the adults. "Looks like we're the first ones to locate any of the horses."

Cheers rang out among the group, and the adults quickened their pace and soon joined the girls at the top of the hill.

"The boys in Miss Schaffer's group will be so jealous that a bunch of girls beat them." A red-haired girl whose name Evan didn't know rubbed her hands together and grinned.

Benny dismounted and looked at Evan. "Could you hold my horse for me? Those horses down there know me, so I'd best approach them on foot alone. You guys stay here so you won't scare them away."

Evan looked at the reins and then the horse. He reached out and took the reins in spite of his nervousness at being so close to an animal with such big teeth. Taylor smiled and walked over. She petted the horse, but an ornery sparkle gleamed in her eye. "You're not afraid of him, are you?"

"No." *Okay, so maybe that was a half-truth. A man's got his pride, after all.* He steeled himself and touched the horse's nose, amazed at its softness. The black horse sniffed his hand, blowing its warm breath across his palm.

"Isn't it cool how God made such big animals, and yet they can be so gentle?" Taylor combed her fingers through the horse's black mane. "I love riding. Can we go again?"

"Yeah, if you want."

Taylor clapped her hands.

The horse jerked his head, and Evan nearly dropped the reins. He shot a warning glance to Taylor, and she giggled. Evan shook his head and patted the horse's neck. He had tolerated the trail ride but had never felt completely comfortable. Still, if it made Taylor happy, he could endure another hour on the back of a horse.

Benny strode down the hill, carrying three lead ropes. He reached into his vest pocket and pulled out some feed, and the nearest horse lifted its head and walked toward him. Benny allowed the horse to eat, then snapped on the lead rope and led the gray horse up the hill toward them. The other horses followed at a good distance.

"Is it true what everybody is saying?" Taylor flicked a strand of her dark hair away from her mouth and gazed up at Evan with clear blue eyes. The wind picked up, blowing her shoulder-length hair in all directions. She grabbed it and held it in place behind her head with one hand.

Evan frowned. "What are they saying?"

"That you saved Miss Schaffer from. . .well, you know."

He should have realized word would have gotten around about him coming to Miss Schaffer's rescue. Evan shrugged. "I was just in the right place at the right time."

Taylor blinked and looked up, something like awe on her face. "God put you there, didn't He?"

"That's what I believe."

The widest grin he'd seen in months brightened Taylor's face. "You're a hero."

She wrapped her arms around him and laid her head against his chest. "Thank you for bringing me here, Uncle Evan. I know you have important work to do, but I really appreciate it."

Before he could respond, she darted toward Benny. Warmth flooded through him as he realized that his sacrifice of time had been worth it.

The horse beside him whinnied as loudly as if someone had blown a trumpet in Evan's ear. He lunged backward three feet and nearly dropped the reins. Chuckles mounted around him.

Evan had never been so out of his comfort zone before, but seeing Taylor so happy and relaxed made all the hassles of this trip well worth it. He just had to keep reminding himself of that.

seven

Bethany set the heated syrup on the serving counter and uncovered the massive pile of pancakes that Jenny had cooked. Teens in hoodies and jackets huddled together at the front of the serving line, chatting and gently shoving one another. Bethany lifted the lid off the sausage and eggs then waved to the leader. The savory scent of grilled sausage filled the air, as well as the odor of fresh coffee. "Come and get it."

She stretched her back to rid it of the kinks and took another sip of her coffee. The screen door screeched as Big Jim strode in and made a beeline for the coffeepot. He swigged down a whole steaming cup and poured another, then turned to face her. He leaned back against the counter, making sure to stay out of Jenny's way.

"Got fresh hotcakes. Want some?" Jenny swiveled her spatula in the air.

Jim smiled. "Sounds good." He pulled out a chair and sat at the table, then heaved a big sigh and looked up.

Bethany's heart jolted. What now? "I looked everything over early this morning, right after Ed woke me with his crowing. Everything seemed fine. I know that look. What's wrong?"

Jim took another sip of coffee and stared at her over his cup. "That computer geek you like is sick."

She sucked in a breath. Evan? He'd been fine the day before. "What's wrong with him? And I never said I liked him."

Jim lifted his fuzzy brows and gave her a knowing stare.

"Okay, I like him. He's a nice guy, even if he's a bit weird. How bad is he?" She glanced at the power strip, and her heart stumbled. Evan hadn't recharged his laptop batteries.

"Fever. Headache."

She rested her forehead on her palms and gripped her hair. What could he have? She peeked over her shoulder at the line of guests filling their plates. Was it contagious? "Is anyone else sick?"

Jim shrugged. "Not that I know of. His roommate, Mr. Perry, I think, came and got me. Wanted to know if we had any medicine."

Bethany stood. "There's some acetaminophen in the medicine chest. I can take it to him."

Jim smirked and lifted one brow.

She straightened and stared him in the eye. "I'm the boss's daughter, so it's only right that I check on him."

"Uh-huh." Jim sipped his coffee.

Jenny smacked down a plate of food in front of him. "You leave her alone, you big ox."

Jim chuckled and cut his pancakes with his fork. He got up and helped himself to the syrup then sat down again. "You know someone will have to take him back, so that means we can't move the wagons again."

Bethany shook her head and looked at Jenny. "We're okay on food, right?"

The cook nodded. "I think so. I'll check the inventory after breakfast and call you if I need anything; then you can bring it when you come back."

"All right, I'll go check out our patient. Jim, can you come up with something different for the guests to do today? They all seemed to enjoy hunting for the horses yesterday."

"Yeah, I'll set up the volleyball nets and get out the ball equipment. Maybe see if I can get an adults versus kids game going. That always stirs up interest, but if that doesn't work, we'll have a fishing tournament."

Bethany got the pills from the medicine kit and grabbed a can of pop. Outside of Evan Parker's tent, she halted. She'd cleaned the tents plenty of times but had never gone in when one of the guests was present. Through the netting of the door, she could see a shadowy bundle on the back cot. Nobody else was around. She cleared her throat. "Mr. Parker, it's Bethany Schaffer. May I come in? I have some medicine for you."

He groaned, threw back the blanket, sat up, and dropped the cover over his lap. "Yeah."

His voice sounded croaky. She slipped inside and pulled a chair close to his bed. His head hung down, resting in his hands, and he looked cute in his University of Wyoming sweatshirt with his hair all messed up. He scratched his chest and looked up.

Bethany's heart melted. At first she'd thought maybe he was just sunburned from spending the day outside without a hat, but his eyes held pain. She reached out and touched his forehead. "You've got a fever."

"That stinks."

Her lips tilted up. "I brought you something that might help." She opened the bottle of acetaminophen and handed two of them to him. His hand felt hot as her fingers touched his palm. She popped the lid of a can of 7UP and gave it to him. He stuck the pills in his mouth and took a drink, then passed the can back to her.

"Thanks."

"Do you think you could eat anything?"

He swayed then scooted under the covers and lay down. "No."

"Besides a fever, are you sick to your stomach? Do you hurt anywhere else?"

He stuck an arm under his pillow. "My head and back ache."

Maybe he had a virus, but it could be something more serious. She remembered the boy who had been here the year she turned sixteen. He'd had a low-grade fever and a stomachache. Nothing major, but after a few days, his mother insisted they go to town to see a doctor. The boy had appendicitis, and the doctor told his mother that he could have died if his appendix had ruptured. Since then they'd taken no chances. If someone got sick, he or she returned to the ranch.

Bethany stared at the man. Even with a day's growth of his dark beard and his eyes shut, something about him tugged at her. But it was his sky blue eyes that took her breath away— them and his kindness. Evan scratched his chest.

"Why do you keep scratching?"

"I itch." His mouth cocked up in a weak grin.

"Let me see your chest."

His lids lifted halfway, and his brows arched.

"Mr. Parker. . ."

"Evan."

Bethany sighed but secretly smiled. "Evan, there are things out here that you don't encounter in the city, and some people are highly allergic to them."

He shoved the blanket away and lifted his sweatshirt. Bethany resisted gasping out loud. Angry red spots dotted his flat stomach and mixed with the brown hair on his chest. What in the world? *I've got to get him back home.*

She indicated for him to pull down his shirt. "You rest, and I'm going to make arrangements to take you back to the ranch. You need to have a doctor check you over."

"I can't go. This trip means too much to Taylor." He shook his head. "I'll be better tomorrow."

She rested her hand on his arm. "Maybe, but we can't take a chance that what you have could be contagious. You need to be isolated."

"I'll stay here, in this tent."

She shook her head. "You would still have to use the bathroom facilities, and besides, you seem too weak to even walk that far."

"I'll manage," he growled.

Bethany stood, distancing herself from him. "I'm sorry, but for your own well-being, we can't let you stay."

He ran his hand through his hair. "Taylor will be so disappointed."

"Let me see what I can do." It was normally against ranch policy for a child to be there without a parent or guardian, but maybe Taylor could stay with another family. Bethany strode across the campground, half angry with herself. Why was she willing to bend the rules for Evan Parker's niece when she wouldn't do it for someone else?

Taylor hurried toward her, carrying a plate of food. Her brows lifted when she saw Bethany leaving the tent. "I thought I'd see if Uncle Evan could eat something."

"Good luck with that." Bethany smiled. "I don't think he feels up to eating, especially something like sausage."

Taylor glanced down. "Oh, I didn't think of that. Maybe he could eat a little of the eggs."

"Yeah, that might help him. I left a can of pop in the tent and gave him something for his headache and fever." She looked down, steeling herself for the girl's response. "I'm sorry, but we're going to have to take him back to the ranch. We need to get him checked by a doctor. I have no clue what's wrong with him."

Taylor pressed her lips together and stared off toward the mountains. "Yeah, I was afraid of that."

Bethany laid her hand on the girl's arm. "I'm going to see if another parent would be willing to take responsibility for you so you can stay with the tour."

Taylor's eyes sparked for a moment then dulled. "Thanks, but I should stay with my uncle in case he needs me."

"You sure?"

She nodded. "I'll see if I can get him to eat and then start packing our stuff. I guess I just wasn't meant to go on this trip."

"All right, if you're positive. I'm going to call my dad and see if he can get the doctor from town to come and check your uncle."

They parted, and Bethany strode back to the cookhouse. She couldn't help being worried about Evan. Nobody had ever had a rash like that, as far as she could remember. It seemed isolated to his chest, which was odd, since she'd never seen him go anywhere without a shirt. That probably ruled out an allergic reaction.

She thought about her first few meetings with him. Why had she considered him such a geek, just because he lugged his computer around? She smiled. Because he was.

A large crowd of guests sat at the picnic tables, laughing, talking, and devouring their breakfast. *Good, keep things as normal as possible.* Maybe if she hurried, they could get Evan and Taylor away without too many people asking questions. She hoped the Perrys would not get sick since they shared a tent.

Back inside the kitchen, Jenny and Jim stared at her with curiosity. Bethany grabbed the phone. "I'm taking Mr. Parker and his niece back to the ranch."

Jim lifted a brow. "*You're* taking them?"

"Yes. Why don't you see about getting the net up?"

Jim's thick lips twisted into a humorous smirk. "Yes, ma'am. You're the boss."

Bethany stuck out her tongue at him and grinned.

An hour later, she drove the Jeep toward the ranch, taking it slowly so as not to jar Evan too much. He sat beside her, hunched against the door, eyes closed. Every so often her gaze would meet Taylor's concerned one in the rearview mirror.

Bethany had to admit that she admired the girl for sacrificing her trip to stay with her uncle. She hadn't expected the teen to respond in such a mature way. In fact, Bethany realized that she had wrongly judged them both.

Why was that?

She swerved to miss a pothole. She didn't think of herself as an overly judgmental person. For the most part, she liked people.

Barrett Banner invaded her thoughts, and she clenched her jaw. Why would her ex-boyfriend come to mind now?

She glanced over to check on Evan, and it hit her. The men somewhat resembled each other. Barrett was about the same height, around six feet, but he was stockier than Evan. Barrett had been the only man she'd considered marrying— until he dumped her for a redheaded biology major with a cheerleader's body. Her grip tightened on the steering wheel as she remembered Barrett's blue eyes.

Bethany scowled. Had she somehow subconsciously considered the two men the same?

But they weren't, not by a long shot.

Barrett had been a taker, moving in and forcing a relationship she hadn't wanted at first, and then when she decided that she did, he dropped her cold.

She drove into the ranch yard and pulled around to the side entrance so Evan wouldn't have to walk so far. She hadn't known him long, but she couldn't imagine him treating a woman as Barrett had. Too bad she'd never get a chance to find out. Once she got him settled and heard what the doctor had to say, she'd return to the tour and would probably never see Evan Parker again.

❧

The doctor straightened and eyed Evan over the top of his black-rimmed glasses. "Well, Mr. Parker, it seems you have the chicken pox."

Confusion swarmed Evan's already foggy mind. Chicken pox? Hadn't Erin said he'd already had them? "But I thought that was a kids' disease."

"Usually it is, but adults do occasionally get it, and it can be quite severe. Until all your spots crust over, you're highly contagious." He ran a long, thin finger over his mustache and looked around. Evan followed his gaze. The large bedroom sported a king-sized bed, two nightstands with lamps, a recliner on the far side of one nightstand, and a large wardrobe with a television hidden behind double doors. Bear and moose statues accentuated the wallpaper around the top of the walls, which displayed log cabins and woodland creatures.

"You're fortunate to have such a nice suite here. I suggest you stay in your room for the next week or so and take things easy. Enjoy the room service and relax." His expression softened. "I'm sure that's not the vacation you had planned when you came here."

Evan shrugged, but he suddenly realized he'd just been handed hours upon hours in which he could work on his program—just as soon as his raging headache dimmed. *Please, Lord, make it so.*

Of course, that wasn't fair to Taylor. Maybe he could talk her into going back to the tour with Miss Schaffer.

Dr. Franklin scribbled something in his black leather notebook. "When did you first notice the rash, Mr. Parker?"

"Last night when I took a shower." Evan cleared his throat. It hurt, and he longed for something cold to drink.

"Hmm. Since the rash just appeared, I'm going to prescribe an antiviral drug for you to take. It may lessen the severity of your symptoms." Dr. Franklin packed away his instruments and lifted his black bag. He tugged on his gray goatee. "You can expect to have a few uncomfortable days. Calamine lotion may help with the itching, but see to it you don't scratch. It only makes things worse and can cause scarring."

Great. Half of his body itched as if he'd rolled in a poison ivy patch and scratching wasn't allowed. He relaxed against the soft pillow and stuck his hands behind his head. At least he was in a comfortable bed and partway back to civilization.

"Miss Schaffer has my phone number. If you get worse in any way, have her call me. Chicken pox is rare in adults, and it can cause serious complications. Make sure you drink plenty of liquids, and you can take ibuprofen for your headache." He tipped his Western hat and left the room, carrying his worn black bag with him. The man reminded Evan of Doc Adams from *Gunsmoke*, a TV show he'd watched as a kid.

The second the doctor closed the door to their suite, Taylor bolted out of her room and into his.

"Hold it right there, young lady." He dropped his hand back to the bed.

She lifted one hand like a princess and swirled it around. "Oh, I had the chicken pox back when I was in kindergarten, so I'm immune. Let me see your spots."

"No." Evan leaned back against his pillow. Just lifting his head to look at his niece made it throb. "I'm really sorry about this, sweetie."

Taylor sighed and sat on the foot of his bed. "It's not your fault. Like, if it's anybody's, I blame Jamie. He's the one who gave you the chicken pox."

"And who gave them to Jamie?"

She shrugged and sighed. "Got 'em at school, I imagine."

Evan smiled. "So we can blame some nameless fifth grader."

"Yeah, I guess." Taylor's lips turned upward. "So, are you hungry? I could get you something from downstairs."

"Thirsty, and I could use some ibuprofen."

Taylor hopped up as if happy to find something to do. "I'll be right back. You want a Coke?"

"Apple juice or ginger ale if they have it. I might take some soup later." Evan rolled onto his side and stuck a pillow against his stomach. He nudged his chin toward his pants on the desk chair. "Get some money out of my wallet. Get yourself a snack if you want one, and take enough money for what we need now and some for you to have if you want something later."

Someone knocked, and Taylor opened the hallway door. Evan thought he heard Miss Schaffer mumble something but couldn't make out the words. Taylor ambled back into the bedroom. "Bethany wants to see you if it's okay."

He nodded and made sure the hunter green blanket covered most of his body. He saw her shadow moments before she stood at the door with a shy smile on her lips. Her honey-colored hair, which had been blown haphazardly by their Jeep ride earlier, had been tamed once again.

Those dark chocolate eyes stared at him with concern; then her lips danced as if she were holding back a grin. "Chicken pox?"

Evan shrugged. "What can I say? Guilty as charged."

Bethany pressed her lips together, but her eyes still glimmered. She fiddled with the doorjamb with her fingers. "I'm sorry. It's just that when I saw that rash, I thought maybe you were having some horrible allergic reaction to something you came in contact with. Can I get you anything?"

Evan's gaze took in her red cotton shirt tucked into her jeans, revealing her narrow waist and womanly figure. Dust-covered boots completed her outfit, making her look every bit the Western woman she was. "Taylor has money to get me something to drink and for some pills for my head. Maybe you could open the store?"

Bethany nodded and waved her hand in the air. "Of course I can, but get whatever you want. It's on the house. I'm driving to town to get your prescription filled and need to know your birth date and home address. I have your sister's address on record, since she made the reservation, but not yours." Her cheeks reddened. "The pharmacy always asks for that info."

His head felt as if it was caught in a vice, and he longed to scratch his whole body. "Have Taylor show you my driver's license. It's got all that info. Could you maybe pick up some calamine lotion?"

Bethany's golden brows lifted.

"The doc said it would help with the itching."

She smiled, sending his stomach into spasms. Or maybe it was because he hadn't eaten all day. "Sorry to be all this trouble. We'll get out of your hair just as soon as I feel like driving."

"Just get better and don't worry about that."

"Yeah, this is one of those times where we have to trust that God knows what He's doing."

Her smile dimmed, and she waved. "Be back soon."

She left his room but not his mind.

He couldn't help admiring how in-charge she was around the camp and didn't let bugs or critters bother her, but she seemed to get flustered when things didn't go as planned or when he mentioned God. What could have happened to cause such a reaction?

"Lord, help her come to know You. Let Bethany see that You can ease her load if she'll only let You."

eight

Bethany smacked the wheel of her Jeep as she spun onto the highway, squealing her tires and scattering pebbles behind her. She ought to be heading back to camp to see if anyone else had fallen sick, but she needed to pick up Evan's prescription and get him on the road to recovery so he could go home. Still, deep down, if she were honest with herself, she'd admit that she was glad to be able to do something to help him. He'd looked so helpless lying in bed with his hair all messed up and blue eyes filled with discomfort.

He was right about trusting God when things went wrong. She knew that in her heart, but getting her mind to align with that truth was something else. Her father was a tough, quiet man who worked hard. He didn't show affection easily. Bethany rarely saw her parents kiss except for a little good-bye peck, like a bird snatching a crumb. Her dad had always been busy, and after her mother died, it seemed as if he'd worked even harder to drown his sorrow. She'd had to figure things out herself and find answers to her problems rather than relying on her father to help her. When had she quit relying on God, too?

Chicken pox. She shook her head and grinned. She'd never heard of an adult catching that. Suddenly, her smile faded. Had she ever had them?

She couldn't remember, but maybe her dad would know.

The doctor had said Evan already had the chicken pox in his system before he came to Moose Valley—that a person could be contagious before they even knew they had it. What if she had already contracted the disease? She moaned. "Wonderful! Just wonderful."

How many others would come down sick before the end of the tour? She'd better get several bottles of that calamine lotion and keep the doctor's phone number handy.

He had also said that the chicken pox took ten days to two weeks to incubate. That meant it wasn't likely anyone else would come down with it before the end of the tour. Still, she'd need to notify each family that they had been exposed to the disease. But what if a bunch of them wanted to leave and asked for a refund?

Concern chased her like a crazed bull. She guided the Jeep along the road, passing wide valleys of wildflowers, going up and down steep hills and around sharp switchbacks. The drive to town was as pretty as any one would see on the tour, but today her mind was elsewhere.

If she had to, she could use her savings to give partial refunds to a few of the guests, but she hoped it wouldn't come to that. If only Evan Parker hadn't come to Moose Valley. She wouldn't have this worry, and the man wouldn't be bugging her mind like a bad case of the chiggers.

And why was he always on her mind?

Yeah, he was cute and tall. But there was something about him that drew her like a butterfly to a flower. He exuded peacefulness.

She pulled into the pharmacy lot and parked. That was it. While she wrestled with the turmoil of the ranch's finances and the problems on the wagon tour, Evan was calm and peaceful. Never rattled.

Just like her mother had been.

She opened her door and stepped out of the Jeep. Well, maybe that worked for him, but she had an ongoing mystery to solve. It was a good thing she was going back to the tour this afternoon and that Evan Parker would have gone home by the time she returned. Too much peacefulness could drive a woman crazy. She knew that for a fact.

An hour and a half later, Bethany tramped into the lodge and set the sack of medicine on the counter. When you lived so far up in the mountains, there was no such thing as a quick trip to town.

Her dad mumbled something into the office phone and hung up. His chair squeaked as he rolled backward, and then he stood. His warm smile settled her worries as he exited the office and leaned on the counter. "As of this moment, we are filled up for the next tour."

"That's great news." She stretched and rolled her head, working the kinks out of her shoulders. "Have you had any more cancellations?"

He nodded. "Two, but I had a waiting list, and those folks were thrilled to fill the openings."

"Good." She smiled. "I got Mr. Parker's medicine. Hey, have I ever had chicken pox?"

Her dad rubbed his chin and stared at the ceiling. After a moment he nodded. "I think so. I know you had something that caused spots all over you."

"Let's hope it wasn't the measles."

"Why?"

"Because Mr. Parker has the chicken pox."

Her dad fought a grin. "Seriously?"

She nodded and rattled the paper bag. "I'll just run this up to Evan's room; then I'm going to take a shower and head back out to the tour."

Her father shuffled his feet and studied the floor. "Well, about that. . . I think you should stay here in case Mr. Parker needs you."

"What?" Bethany straightened. "Why me?"

He leaned his full weight against the counter and tapped a pencil on a notepad with the Moose Valley logo on it. "I don't know nothin' about caring for sick folks. Besides, Scott is back and needs something to do."

She frowned. "I thought you laid off Scott."

He shook his head and looked confused. "What gave you that idea? His grandma died, so he went home for a week to attend the funeral and spend time with his family."

"Oh, guess I misunderstood. I'm glad he's still around." She thought of the good-natured cowboy who played guitar and led the singing around the evening campfire. When she was younger, she'd wanted to grow up and marry the handsome man, but as she got older, she realized the difference in their years was too great. He was closer to her dad's age than hers.

A playful grin tugged at her dad's lips and danced in his eyes. "Besides, I thought you might like some time to get that fancy computer of yours set up. Not that I'll ever use it once you're gone from here."

Her heart somersaulted, and her mind immediately started assembling the computer. "Really? I'd love to get started on that project."

He slapped the counter so hard that she jumped. "Good! I'll tell Scott to get packed. Are there any supplies we need to take with us?"

"Us?"

"With all the problems this week, I thought it might be good to have an extra set of eyes up there."

She nodded. "Might not be a bad idea. As far as supplies, I don't know of any, but you might call Jenny or Jim. Someone is going to have to survey all the guests and find out if everyone has had the chicken pox. Or at least inform them that they've been exposed."

"What if they haven't? We sure can't offer them all a refund."

Bethany crossed her arms. "I don't know. If they've just now been exposed, then maybe they won't be contagious or break out until they return home. The doc said it takes a week and a half to two weeks to incubate."

Her dad stood and scratched his head with both hands, leaving his short gray hair pointing in a jillion different directions. Kind of like someone else's. "Okay then, I'll go hunt down Scott."

"After you do that, could you get those computer boxes from our living room and cart them down to the office while I get a shower?"

Ever the Western gentleman, he tipped an imaginary hat. "Yes, ma'am. I can do that."

She jogged up the steps, her excitement growing. Finally. She'd be able to bring her family's record-keeping system into the twenty-first century. She slowed her steps outside Evan's suite; the television hummed through the walls. Maybe she could recruit Taylor to help her. The girl must be bored.

She thought of her foreman's daughter. *That's it. I can introduce her to Cheryl.*

She reached up to knock on the door then lowered her hand. If Bethany stayed here, she would probably see more of Evan. She would have to face her feelings instead of running back on tour as she'd planned.

But then what was the point of it? He'd leave in a week and go back to his home in Laramie, and she'd go to Denver. She'd learned years ago that long-distance relationships never worked out. Oh sure, there were sworn promises to e-mail or call, but the longer two people were apart, the rarer those contacts became. Better just to nip things in the bud.

She knocked on the door, and after a moment Taylor answered, eyeing the sack in Bethany's hands. "Hi."

Bethany held it out to her. "I've got your uncle's prescription and calamine lotion. I also picked up a bottle of ibuprofen for him so he can take them as he needs. Is there anything else I can do for you guys?"

Taylor shook her head. Without the sassy teen attitude pouring forth, the girl was pretty with her dark brown hair and blue eyes almost as vibrant as her uncle's.

"Let me set this down and get the money. Uncle Evan said to be sure I paid you for the medicine."

Bethany waited while the girl fished around in her pockets and held out the money. "Thanks."

Taylor leaned against the doorjamb as if in no hurry to get back to her show.

Bethany ought to leave, but she wanted to ask about Evan. "How's he doing?"

"Sleeping, moaning, and trying not to scratch." Taylor grinned. "Men can be such babies when they're sick. Mom always said if Dad got a paper cut on his finger, he'd have to go to bed for two days."

Bethany shared a chuckle with the teen. Her dad had always been hale and hearty, and she knew nothing about men being sick. "I'm going to put together a new computer downstairs. If you get bored and want something to do, feel free to come and help."

Taylor's eyes sparked with interest. "Thanks. I might just do that after I give Uncle Evan his medicine."

Walking down the hall, she thought how fortunate Evan was to have his niece to care for him. The few times she'd been sick, Polly, the ranch cook, had tended to her, but it wasn't the same as having family care for you. Bethany sighed. She wished she could have checked on Evan herself, but it hardly seemed proper now that they were back at the lodge. She ran down the stairs, thankful to have a project that would occupy her mind and rid it of Evan Parker.

꙰

Evan very gently rubbed—not scratched—an itch through his T-shirt. As soon as he quit rubbing, the sore started itching again. Now that the spots had scabbed over, they itched even more. He grabbed the bottle of calamine, put a glob on his finger, and lifted his to shirt to paint the offending area. He looked as if he'd been the loser in a paintball battle against a bunch of girls using pink paint.

Taylor had gone downstairs to chat with a new friend she'd made. Lucky her. There were so many other things he'd rather do besides laying in bed that even chatting sounded fun. Being laid up was kind of like going on a fast. Food he'd rarely eaten, like hot dogs and fish, sounded good. Now, just about anything would be fun. Even the wagon train ride didn't seem so bad. Had Bethany returned there? He hadn't seen her since the day he came back to the lodge.

But hadn't Taylor mentioned something about helping her put together a new computer? The days swam into one, and he couldn't remember much about the past few, but now that his head was clearing, he needed to try to get some work done.

He glanced at the bird clock on the wall. The incessant chirping every hour on the hour had driven him crazy until he'd finally crawled out of bed and removed the batteries. Sure, it looked great with the room's decor, but it was annoying.

His stomach growled, reminding him that dinnertime was just an hour away. A woman named Polly had delivered meals to him the past few days, but Taylor had met Polly's daughter, Cheryl, and decided to eat downstairs with her.

He glanced at his pink-splotched belly. With his sores healing, he was no longer contagious, and fortunately, none had formed on his face. Maybe he could clean up and eat downstairs this evening and then get some work done on his project tonight. He stood and made his way to the bathroom. If he hurried, he just might surprise Taylor and Miss Schaffer.

An hour later Evan sat back in his chair in the dining hall. "You have no idea how good it feels to leave that room."

"I know I sure got tired of it until I met Cheryl. She's a lot of fun." Taylor took a sip of her pop and followed it with the final bite of apple pie. "Mmm, that was really good. I'm going to the barn and see if Cheryl's there. She said I could help her brush down the horses this evening. Then we're going swimming."

Evan leaned forward. "I know it's summer, but isn't it a bit too cool for swimming after the sun sets?"

Taylor grinned and stood. "The pool is heated."

"Be careful around those horses. They're—big." He shivered at the thought of his niece anywhere close to those big teeth and hooves, but she'd occupied most of her time down at the barn while he recuperated. Now he understood better what Erin went through watching her oldest child grow up and away from her.

Taylor put her tray on the conveyor belt, and it rolled into the kitchen. She dashed out a side door. Evan knew she'd been surprised to see him downstairs and even a bit relieved. Silverware clinked at the few tables with guests, and the soft buzz of conversation floated around the room. A wide two-story window offered a magnificent view of the mountains. If he had to be stuck somewhere recovering, this place was much better than most.

"Well, look who decided to rejoin the living." Bethany stood beside him holding a tray of food.

His heart did a little flip-flop. "Yeah, I'm AAK."

"What?"

"AAK—Alive and kicking."

"Oh, I get it. Geek speak. Mind if I join you?"

He waved his hand toward a chair. "Not at all."

She set down her tray, took a seat, and stared at him. "You're not contagious anymore, are you?"

"The doc said I could be in public once all the sores had scabbed over, and they have."

She wrinkled her nose and grabbed the salt shaker. "Such lovely dinner talk."

He sat with one arm over the back of his chair and watched her eat. Her hair was pulled back in one of those stretchy bands, but rebellious wisps hung enticingly around her tanned cheeks. She glanced down to cut her steak, and her long lashes fanned across her cheeks. Evan sighed. Too bad he wouldn't be here much longer.

She peered up at him, an ornery smile making her eyes glisten. "You look like you had a wreck with a Pepto-Bismol truck."

"It's not that pink, is it?" He held out his hand. Several healing sores were covered with pink lotion, and he knew the ones on his neck also showed. "If I was smart, I'd invest in calamine lotion stock."

She giggled and forked another bite into her mouth. After chewing and taking a drink of her tea, she glanced up. "Can I ask you something?"

"Sure."

"I've been trying to figure out ways to better market Moose Valley and come up with more activities to draw people here. We've had some cancellations lately, but I have no clue why. I thought maybe if we had more to offer. . ."

"Well, let me think for a minute." He focused on activities since he knew little about marketing. After a few minutes, he leaned forward. "At the county fair, they had a hot air balloon that people paid to ride in."

She scowled and wiped her mouth with her napkin. "Sounds like a lawsuit waiting to happen."

"Not really. It was tethered. People just rode up, had about a fifteen-minute look around, and came back down."

"What about on windy days?"

"You leave it tied down on the ground."

"Hmm. . .it might work. What did they charge?"

"Fifteen dollars for fifteen minutes—per person." Evan took a sip of his pop and crushed the empty can. "You could even get a balloon made with the ranch's logo on it."

Her eyes sparkled. "I *love* that idea. Wonder how much something like that would cost."

He shrugged. "No clue."

Evan pushed his tray to the center of the table and leaned his arms where it had been. "Do you ever open the place up for guests in the winter?"

She shook her head. "No. It's too hard for tourists to get here when the snow is deep."

"Well, maybe you should rethink that. You could offer sleigh rides and maybe some winter sports."

She smiled at a couple who walked past their table. "I'll have to think on that for a while. I'm not sure we want people here in the winter, not that I plan to be here."

"Where would you be?"

She fiddled with her cup of tea then finally looked up. "I have a job in Denver that I'm supposed to start in another week."

Evan felt his brows tug upward. "You're leaving the ranch?"

She was silent so long that he didn't think she'd answer. "It's been a dream of mine for a long time."

"Wow." He looked around the large dining hall and out at the mountains, their snowy tops glistening in the sun. "I can't imagine living in a place like this and just walking away from it. It's like being five thousand feet closer to God."

She pursed her lips and heaved a breath through her nose. Then she stood. "Yeah, well, just imagine how lonely this place is when there's nobody around for months on end. And try making new friends, only to watch them leave every few weeks."

She snatched up her tray and stormed away.

"Wow. Did I ever hit a sore spot." He'd never thought about it before, but even with so many people around, Bethany Schaffer was lonely. How could she not be when everyone she met stayed only a few days to a few weeks and then was gone from her life like snow under the summer sun?

nine

Bethany pursed her lips. Setting up the new computer was proving to be more complicated than she'd expected. Once she and Taylor had unloaded everything from the boxes, there had been a plethora of wires to connect, not to mention making room on the counter for the monitor and keyboard. She tapped a pencil against the granite counter and waited for the professional accounting software to install. The printer that her college roommate had given her had saved some money, but it didn't match the rest of the equipment. Oh well, who would even notice?

"Hey, you got a computer."

Bethany peered up into Evan's eager blue eyes, and her limbs felt as boneless as spaghetti. The pencil flipped out of her fingers and rolled across the counter. She owed him an apology for storming out after dinner last night. He was just being friendly, but he'd hit too close to home.

"So, are you working the registration desk *and* the gift shop?" He glanced at the store. "I need a caffeine fix."

"There's free coffee in there." She nudged her chin toward the open doors of the dining hall.

Evan scrunched up his lips in a cute way and waved a hand in the air. "I've never had a cup of coffee. Can't stand the taste."

"If you've never had any, how do you know you don't like it?" Bethany eased off the stool she'd been sitting on.

He grinned wide, revealing even, white teeth. Her stomach felt as if a flock of butterflies were trying to escape. "Okay, so

I tried it in college. Once." He grimaced and shuddered. "I just prefer my caffeine cold."

She chuckled at his performance, grabbed the key to the gift shop, then opened the door. She needed a break anyway. "A cold drink sounds good."

Inside the store, Evan opened the small refrigerator's door and grabbed a can. He looked back over his shoulder. "What's your pleasure, ma'am? I'm buying."

"You don't have to do that."

He lifted up a hand, silencing her. "What kind do you want? Or should I just pick?"

She sighed. "Root beer, please."

He snagged a brown can and meandered along the row of candy bars.

"Are you one of those junk food addicts?"

His head was lowered as he studied the selection. His hair looked more orderly than normal. "Guilty as charged." He chose two bars and plunked them on the counter with the pop cans. He reached into his pocket and pulled out a five-dollar bill.

Bethany rang up his purchase and handed him his change.

"Care to join me on the porch for a few minutes?" he asked.

She had plenty of work to do, but until the computer was finished doing its thing, she was at a standstill. "Just let me check the progress of the software I'm installing, and I'll take a short break."

With the program at just forty-seven percent loaded, she figured she might have five minutes to spend with Evan. She dashed into the office, grabbed a brush from the top drawer, and ran it through her hair. She wasn't primping for him, she fibbed to herself.

Outside, Evan had pulled two of the wooden rockers close together. Her root beer lay on the seat of the empty chair. She snatched it up and sat down, popping the top of the can. It hissed and sizzled, sending a sweet scent into the air. The snowcapped mountains rose up before them. She'd grown so accustomed to seeing them that she pretty much took the view for granted. She needed to take time to appreciate the beauty around her—and the heritage that would one day belong to her.

"Choose one." Evan held out the two candy bars.

"Oh, no thanks. This drink is plenty."

He tossed one at her then tore the paper off the other and started eating. Bethany grabbed at the bar as it slid down her leg. "You don't take no for an answer, do you?"

He shrugged, giving her a charming look. Maybe he wasn't as unaware of his appeal as she'd first thought. She tore back the paper and bit into the sweet confection.

"Are you planning on putting your registration system on your computer now that you have one?"

She took a drink of her pop and peered at him. "We've had a computer for a while, but it's an older one. We keep it in our private quarters. But yes, I do hope to get the registration on the new computer soon, although I plan to install the bookkeeping program first."

"That should make things much easier for you and will save time."

"That's what I'm hoping." She bit off a small piece of her chocolate bar.

"You know, that printer you have isn't going to work with your new operating system."

Bethany nearly choked on a peanut and leaned forward, coughing. Evan patted her back and looked concerned. She washed the bite down with a drink of root beer, thinking about the money she'd saved by not buying a printer. "Why not?"

"Those new operating systems don't have drivers for printers as old as yours."

"That's just great."

"The dealer should have explained it when you bought your computer. Basically, the manufacturers wanted people to have to buy more printers, so they didn't write a printer driver that would allow older printers to work on the new system."

"The clerk asked if I needed one, but I told him I already had one." She leaned back, allowing the view to comfort her.

He fiddled with his can then looked at her. "I saw your Web site. It's a nice, basic one. I, uh. . .wouldn't mind designing a fancier one for you—as a way of saying thanks for allowing me to stay here and for caring for me while I was sick."

Bethany waved her hand in the air. "Thanks, but that's not necessary."

He lifted up his rocker and jiggled it around to face her. "No, seriously. I'm a computer engineer. Designing a Web site would be simple. I like doing it, and maybe a fancier one would help draw more business to your place."

Their Web site was plain but functional. She'd designed it using a basic template that the Web host offered. If they redid it, they could add pictures and all kinds of features. Hope building, she reconsidered. "Could you maybe add one of those animations? Like a moving wagon train or a galloping horse?"

His wide grin warmed her insides, and she was glad that the chicken pox hadn't marred his fine features. "You bet. Or we could videotape a real wagon and show the mountains behind it. Maybe even with the sun setting."

Excitement growing, she jumped up. "Let me get some paper and make notes."

Evan stood and followed her inside the lodge and behind the registration desk. "I could take some pictures with my digital camera to show the awesome countryside and the main lodge. Might even take a photo of that old tree trunk with the mother and baby bear carving, with the stairs to the lodge in the background."

Bethany checked the monitor. "My accounting software's done loading, but let's work on the Web site idea. I'd love to have a site that lists our prices and shows everything we have to offer."

She pulled a pad of paper from a drawer and grabbed a pencil. She wrote down several items then tapped her pencil against the paper as she considered what else to add. Since Evan was more than willing to build a new Web site, she wanted the best one possible.

❧

Evan couldn't help smiling. Once she'd decided to proceed with the new Web site, Bethany jumped in with both feet. Standing beside him, her chin rested in one hand with her elbow on the counter, her other shoulder pressed against his. She'd leaned in at one point and never moved away.

He liked her nearness and the feel of her arm touching his. Wisps of blond hair flittered around her tanned cheeks. She was organized, reliable, cute, and lively—when she wasn't worrying about everything. And she'd been very kind and nurturing when he'd first become sick. He knew then that he wanted to get to know her better. To have a relationship with her.

But as an unbeliever, she was off-limits. He sidestepped and put some distance between them, not that four inches was all that much. At least she was no longer touching him.

He zeroed in on the notepad and refocused on the job at hand. If he could get the basics of what she wanted, he could hide himself back in his room and get to work. This job should only take a few hours.

He cleared his throat. "I can add a counter if you like. That way you will know how many hits you're getting and where the visitors live."

She turned those doelike eyes on him. "You can do that? Tell where people live?"

He nodded and forced himself to look away. His heart pounded, and he watched myriad dust motes floating along on a beam of sunlight. Picking up his pop can, he moistened his dry mouth.

"That's about all I can come up with," Bethany said. "What do you think?"

Evan forced his gaze back to the notepad. "Looks good. What would you like for your dominant colors?"

Her gaze roved the lodge. "I guess we should stick with woodland colors: brown and dark green mainly."

"Great." He tore off the top sheet with all her notes. "I'll get started on this right away and have a prototype for you to view by dinnertime."

"That's wonderful. I never dreamed when I got up this morning that we might have a whole new Web site by evening. I don't know how to thank you." She stared into his eyes.

Warning bells went off as he longed to embrace her. He cleared his throat. "I, um. . .can't work on my project until I hear back from my boss and he approves of the section I just completed, so I might as well get started on this now."

She smiled shyly up at him. "All right. I'm anxious to see it."

His gaze lowered to her lips, and he felt as if a mainframe computer rested on top of his chest. *"Submit yourselves, then, to God. Resist the devil, and he will flee from you."*

Okay, so Bethany wasn't the devil, but she was a temptation. She licked her lips, and his heart stumbled. He may be a geek, but he was still a man—a man who'd spent little time with a member of the opposite sex, especially one who intrigued him so much.

Using every ounce of strength left in his body after nearly a week's illness, Evan stepped back. "If I get done before dinner, I'll come down and show you what I've worked up."

She nodded, looking confused. Maybe she'd felt a similar

attraction to him. Thinking that did not help. Not one bit.

He strode toward the elevator, grateful when the thick metal doors closed and blocked his view of Bethany Schaffer. If not for Taylor wanting to stay the full two weeks, he would pack up and be gone as soon as he finished the Web site. But he owed his niece that much.

He'd just have to find a way to steer clear of the tempting Miss Schaffer until then.

ten

The phone jingled, and Bethany picked up the receiver. "Moose Valley Ranch."

"This is Marilyn Bochner. My family has a reservation for your July 19th tour. I need to cancel that."

Bethany's mouth went dry; she clutched the receiver. "May I ask why?"

"It doesn't really matter. We aren't going to be able to come. I understand there's no penalty for canceling. Is that correct?"

Disappointment and the loss of income made Bethany's stomach swirl. "Yes, ma'am. That's right."

"Good. Now, please cancel my reservation."

"Just a minute, please. I need to find your information card." She put the woman on hold and closed her eyes. That was the second cancellation this afternoon. What was going on?

Digging around in the old file box, she located Mrs. Bochner's index card, which had her contact info and reservation date on it. The reservation was for a family of five. Ouch. With tours costing over fifteen hundred dollars per person, Moose Valley was taking a big hit. They definitely needed a cancellation policy. She made a big X across the card and stuck it in back with the terminated reservations, and then she erased the Bochner name from the July 19th tour list.

She picked up the phone and forced a smile into her voice. "All right, ma'am. I've taken care of everything. I hope in the future you might consider trying us again."

The phone clicked without so much as a thank-you from the woman. Bethany exhaled so hard that she fluttered a sticky note that clung to the counter. Why were so many people canceling on short notice? Sure, it happened now and then because emergencies occurred, but not this frequently.

The spicy-sweet scent of barbecue wafted from the dining room, reminding her that dinnertime had arrived. The elevator opened, and Evan shuffled out carrying his laptop. He almost looked as if he were afraid to approach her, as if she wouldn't like his creation.

"How's the Web site coming?"

"Ready for you to approve—or not." He laid the computer on the counter. "Where's your Internet hookup?"

She pointed under the counter, and he plugged in his cord. They'd had the lodge wired for Internet several years back, but she'd never been able to talk her dad into getting a computer for the reservation system and bookkeeping. She'd finally just decided to buy one and make him learn to live with it, and she was glad now that she had. If nothing else, it gave her something in common with Evan.

He logged on and waited for the Internet to come up. His eyes narrowed, and he peered sideways at her. "You know, you really ought to consider getting a wireless setup."

"I'm counting my blessings as it is, just having a computer. Things move slower up in the mountains than in the lowlands. When I was little, we didn't even have electricity."

Evan shook his head and typed in her Web address. "I'd be out of work without that."

Bethany gasped as a beautiful home page filled the screen. An image of the Alpine lodge with the mountains in the background created a masthead with the ranch name in letters that looked as if they'd been created out of pine boards. "It's awesome! Where did you get that picture?"

Evan studied her face as if to gauge her response. "I took it." He leaned close to the screen and pointed at something. "It's real small, but you can see the bear statue right there."

She leaned closer, and sure enough, there it was.

"I have a bigger picture of it on a different page. So, what do you think?"

Glancing up at his boyishly expectant expression, she wanted to lean in and hug him, but she didn't. "I love it so far. Show me more."

"Once we videotape the wagons moving with the mountains in the background, I'll add that here." He pointed to a blank area. "If you want, you or your dad could even narrate the video and tell people about your ranch."

"Dad might enjoy doing that. Besides, he's the real-deal rancher and would draw people's interest."

"We can add more links. I wasn't sure what all you might need. I've made pages for the wagon tours, horseback riding, directions, and your rates, which I need to get from you."

"One thing I do want to add is a cancellation policy. For some reason, we've been getting a lot of them lately."

"Really?" Evan straightened. "You mean more than normal?"

She nodded and clicked on the wagon tours link. "Yeah."

"Do you have the cancellation policy written down? If so, give me a copy, and that will be easy to add."

She turned to face him. "Well, that's the problem. We've never had one. Dad wanted to keep things simple for our guests, and he thought the friendly thing to do was not to have one. We discussed it last night and decided we were losing too much money, so we just came up with one."

"That's probably a smart idea, and you ought to have a nonrefundable deposit. That would make people less likely to cancel." He leaned against the counter. "Just give me the info, and I'll make a cancellation section below the rates."

She pulled the paper from her pocket and studied it. She hated being such a stickler about things, but they couldn't afford to get stuck with empty wagons when they normally had a waiting list.

Evan tapped his index finger against his front tooth and looked deep in thought. She laid the paper on the counter beside him and clicked on another link. Evan sure knew his stuff. This Web site was way more than she ever could have hoped for. He was kind to put so much effort into it.

A movement outside the window snagged her attention. Taylor and Cheryl bumped shoulders and giggled as they climbed the front steps to the lodge. Cheryl held the door for Evan's niece, and the girls ambled toward them. Where Taylor was a willowy brunette, Cheryl was blond, short, and a bit on the chunky side.

Pulled from his thoughts, Evan looked up and smiled at the girls. "Long time, no see."

"So, the patient has emerged from his recovery room again. It's good to see you back among the living." Taylor set her elbows on the counter and rested her chin in her hands. "So, what are you doing back there?"

"Your sweet uncle made a new Web site for us."

Cheryl glanced sideways at Taylor. Both girls had ornery expressions on their faces. "Sweet, huh?"

Bethany realized her error. "Well. . .it was sweet of him to design the site, especially after he's been so sick."

Taylor straightened. "I for one am glad he found something to do. He was about to drive me crazy. Why is it men are such babies when it comes to being sick?"

"I wasn't a baby." Evan looked insulted.

Bethany smiled and patted his shoulder. "It's okay. You had a good reason to be fussy."

"How about buying us something to drink, Uncle Evan?" Taylor lifted her brows expectantly.

"Sure, if the store is open."

Bethany grabbed the key and wiggled it in the air. "Always, for a paying customer."

She walked behind the counter and through the hallway toward the store. The others followed, and Evan mumbled something.

She opened the door and held it back for them to enter. The girls skipped in and bounced over to the pop fridge. Evan ambled in after them, his head down.

"What did you say?" Bethany asked.

His gaze darted up and collided with hers. He stifled a laugh and broke eye contact. "Nothing. Just that I wasn't fussy."

Bethany chuckled under her breath and slid behind the cash register.

&

Outside, Evan sat on the porch with Taylor and Cheryl. The two girls giggled and chattered like magpies. After a few moments, they turned to face him.

"You ought to see how well Taylor can ride a horse now, Mr. Parker."

"Yeah, I'm turning into a regular cowgirl. I'm actually glad you got sick so we had to come back."

"Me, too." Cheryl smiled; then her eyes widened. "I mean, I'm not glad you got sick, but I am glad that Taylor is here."

Evan chuckled.

Taylor tilted her head back and took a drink of bottled water. In the porch lighting, he could see that her skin was darkening, and her cheeks held a healthy, rosy glow. She seemed happier than she had been in months.

"Cheryl's even teaching me how to rope. Do you want to come and see me?"

"I'd like that, but the sun has already set. How about we wait until tomorrow?"

Cheryl popped up from her rocker and glanced at her watch.

"Uh-oh, I'm in trouble. Mom'll be wanting me home since it's getting late. See you tomorrow, Taylor. Thanks for the pop, Mr. Parker."

Taylor watched Cheryl trot to the side of the lodge. The girl waved as she headed toward the cabin she shared with her parents. Taylor turned back and looked at him. "This place sure is peaceful. No traffic sounds, no sirens."

"No teenagers playing their car stereos as loud as they can."

Taylor snickered. "Everybody has an MP3 player now."

"Excuse me for being an old geezer," Evan teased, even though he had his own MP3 player in his room.

Taylor laughed out loud. "You're not that old, Uncle Evan." Her blue eyes twinkled and dark brows waggled up and down. "At least Miss Schaffer doesn't think so."

Evan tightened his grip on the chair. Had Bethany noticed his interest? He'd tried to keep from letting his attraction to her show. He was a city boy and she was a country gal. There was no future for them as a couple. "What do you mean?"

Taylor elbowed him in the arm and grinned. "She likes you. Can't you tell?"

Evan laid his head back against the rocker. He had noticed that the impatience and irritation present in Bethany's gaze when he first met her had dimmed, and her defensive shields had lowered. He *had* noticed her interest in him, but he'd thought her softening was merely gratitude because he'd helped her several times. But maybe there was more to her actions than he'd realized.

He ran his hand through his hair and pushed thoughts of Bethany Schaffer aside. He pulled his gaze away from the darkening mountains and back to Taylor. "It's great to see you smiling again."

She leaned back and crossed her arms. "I like it here. I can't imagine how wonderful it would be to live here."

"You'd get bored. No malls. No movie theaters. No ice cream shops."

"I can get ice cream from Cheryl's mom or in the store."

"Ah, but it's not the same thing."

"If I lived here, I wonder if Mom would let me get a horse of my own."

Evan didn't want to throw cold water on the fires of her dreams, but nothing would come of such thinking. "I'm just glad you're having a good time, sweetie."

"I am. Cheryl's dad is taking us fishing tomorrow." Taylor nibbled her lip. "I can go, can't I?"

That she was asking him and not telling him meant they'd crossed an invisible barrier somewhere along the way. "As long as you're careful and he doesn't mind you tagging along."

The cool evening breeze whipped across his face, bringing with it the fragrant scent of pine. A lodgepole pine on the other side of the parking lot waved its limbs as if in praise to God. How was it that he felt closer to the Lord out here, away from the city?

"Do you think Dad would have stayed with us if we'd lived somewhere like this?"

Evan clenched his jaw as anger surged through him at the way Clint Anderson had hurt his family. He leaned forward and placed his hand on Taylor's arm. "No, sweetie, I don't. Your dad loved your mother and you kids, but he was never one to settle down."

She swiped at the tears on her cheeks. "I used to think it was my fault. That he left because I was bad or something."

Evan stood. He pulled his niece up and into his arms and kissed the top of her head. "Nothing you did caused him to leave. Trust me. He just wasn't a man who could handle responsibility well."

Taylor's tears dampened his shirt, and she clung to him.

"Why couldn't he be more like you?"

Joy flooded Evan's heart. She'd just given him the ultimate—albeit indirect—compliment. He squeezed her tight. "God knows how you feel, Taylor. You can always talk to Him and cry on His shoulder if I'm not there."

She ducked her head and stepped back. She wiped her face and then looked up. "Thanks. I don't know why I suddenly had that meltdown. Maybe because I'm jealous that Cheryl's dad is so nice and friendly."

"Well, I'm not a dad, but you can use my shoulder anytime you need it."

"Thanks."

She smiled, and he wrapped his arm around her shoulder. "I don't know about you, but I'm hungry. Let's go see if there's any pie left over from dinner."

eleven

The elevator doors opened, and Evan turned left toward the registration desk instead of the dining hall. His stomach rumbled in complaint as he sniffed the scents wafting up from the lunch buffet. Burgers would be his guess. After being sick and then getting back on normal food, he'd been amazed at the flavor of the beef served at Moose Valley. He'd never tasted fresh beef raised locally before, and he seriously considered asking about buying some to take home with him.

Bethany leaned down, looking at something on the monitor, and her hair hung around her face, blocking his view of her pretty features. He liked it down much better than pulled back with one of those elastic bands wrapped around it. Her loose purple top hinted at her womanly shape and hung down over her jean-clad legs.

"Hey." He leaned his arms on the counter.

She slowly looked up, and dark chocolate eyes met his. Something in them sparked, spinning his insides in circles, and she smiled. "You won't believe this. We've already had twenty-two hits just since the new Web site went online last night, and I've received two reservations for next month. One visitor was from New York, and another was from Vancouver. Isn't that amazing?"

The expression on her face was amazing. Evan returned her smile, glad that he'd been able to help. He liked making her happy. "Yeah, it is. You might even have to add some more wagons if this keeps up."

She swatted her hand in the air. "Yeah, sure."

"I'm serious. I've got something I want to talk to you about. Can you take a lunch break?"

She glanced into the vacant office behind her. The chair was shoved back, and the new computer boxes still littered the floor. She closed the door, hiding the mess. "I usually watch the desk when Dad's not here, but I guess I could if we eat out here or sit in the dining hall so I can see the desk. You never know when someone will want something."

She walked beside him into the dining room and toward the buffet line. He wished he had the right to hold her hand, but he didn't, and she'd probably go ballistic if he tried in front of her guests. Several tables held families who were staying at the lodge or awaiting the next wagon tour. Taylor sat with Cheryl and her father near the two-story window that showcased the mountains. Both teens seemed to be talking at once and waving their forks at each other. Girls sure were strange at times. If he ever had kids, he'd only have boys. They were much easier to handle and understand.

Evan handed Bethany a tray, then they each gathered their silverware and moved down the line. He took a thick beef patty and topped his bun with mayonnaise, lettuce, and pickles. Bethany slathered hers with mustard and ketchup, then put two slices of cheese on it and added every condiment offered *except* pickles. He shook his head. They were polar opposites in more than one way.

Bethany waved at the cook, who was in the kitchen slicing a pie. It wasn't butterscotch from the looks of it, but he knew it would be tasty, as everything else he'd eaten at Moose Valley had been—except for the meat that had been tampered with. Why would someone want to cause trouble at Moose Valley? It would take a lot of effort to come to such an isolated place and to hang around without being noticed, just waiting for an opportunity to stir up trouble.

They sat down at a table where they had full view of the registration desk. Around them the soft buzz of conversation and the clink of silverware filled the room. Evan said a quick prayer of thanks and closed his eyes as he bit into the thick beef patty. "Mmm. . .this is the best meat I've ever eaten."

A soft smile tilted Bethany's lips. "Yeah, that's one of the things I miss when I'm not here."

"I know you guys raise cattle, since we've seen a lot around here, but who do you sell the meat to?"

"Dad has some contracts with stores and restaurants in nearby towns, but most of what we raise stays here."

He took a swig of his pop. "Have you ever thought about making your beef available to your guests?"

Her brow crinkled then lifted. "Just what do you think you're eating?"

"That's not what I mean." He popped a chip into his mouth. "What if you sold packaged beef to your guests?"

She shook her head. "I don't see how that would work. Most of them fly to Jackson and then rent a car to drive here."

"So? You could ship it to them."

Bethany gave him a patronizing stare. It was the same look Erin gave him whenever he tried to talk computers with her. As if he were dumb to even bring up the subject.

"It can be done. There are companies that specialize in shipping meat to customers."

She stirred her baked beans. "Sounds like a lot of work."

He shook his head. "Not really. You just have to have some of the beef packaged in specific weights. Maybe like five-pound or two-pound packages."

"Well, that works for ground beef but not cuts like steaks."

He shrugged. "I didn't work out all the details, but it seems to me you could stand to make some decent money from such a venture."

She glanced toward the desk then leaned back in her chair and crossed her arms.

"The customers could pay for the shipping cost and the packing. All you'd have to do is box up the meat, invest in some dry ice or frozen packets, and deliver the boxes to a shipper. Sounds pretty simple."

"Uh-huh, and someone has to keep track of those orders and record the information."

"Yeah, there's that." He took another bite of his burger, realizing that there was more involved than he'd first thought.

She leaned forward, arms on the table, eyes focused on his. "You know, you may be on to something. I'll talk to Dad about it tonight."

"I have another idea, too. You want to hear that one?"

Bethany grinned. "I thought you said you didn't know anything about marketing."

"I don't really." He fiddled with his fork, trying to look nonchalant when he felt anything but that. Why was helping her so important to him?

"So. . .what other ideas do you have?"

"I noticed that you don't have any souvenir items with your logo on them."

"Dad never liked the idea of forcing folks to buy stuff like that when they pay so much money to come here."

"Many parents go looking for souvenirs to get for their kids. It's not forcing if they want them. Kids would love little stuffed animals like they see on the wagon tours—moose, deer, beaver, and maybe even a bear."

She sat up straight. "You saw a bear?"

He grinned. "No, but I sure thought about them and how that tent canvas wouldn't keep one out if it wanted in."

"Just so you don't worry, we've rarely had problems with them—not during the summer anyway. The smell of so many people usually keeps them away."

"Usually?"

She lifted one shoulder. "We did have a bear—at least that's what we think it was—break into one of the cookhouses in May. I guess the bear must have smelled food, although we hadn't equipped the cookhouse yet for this summer's tours. It sure made a mess."

Evan tapped on the table, his thoughts running rampant. "What if it wasn't a bear and was the same person who's been causing trouble?"

She opened her mouth then slammed it shut. "I never even considered that, but in light of the problems we've had lately, I probably should."

He laid his hand on her arm. "I'm praying that you'll figure it all out."

"Thanks." She pulled away and leaned against her chair. "Back to your great ideas. Got any more?"

"You might consider having some T-shirts, sweatshirts, or jackets for sale with your logo on them. You could even keep a small stock of those at the cookhouses, so if someone should find out they left their jacket in the car"—he grinned—"they could buy something to keep warm."

"Are you talking about yourself?"

"Maybe."

Bethany shook her head. "You're something else, you know it?"

He wasn't sure if that was a good thing or not, but she *was* smiling. The phone at the registration desk beeped, and Bethany jumped up and ran toward it. He carried their trays to the conveyor belt and set them down. They disappeared under a dark green flap. Spinning around, he noticed Taylor was gone and strode out of the dining room. Now that he was well again, he ought to do a better job of watching her, but Bethany had assured him that Cheryl was very mature for her age and would see to it that Taylor didn't get into trouble. He needed to get back to work. They'd be leaving in a few days, and he was still behind on his project after being sick. His steps slowed as he reached the front desk.

"I can't believe that. Who was it?" Bethany said into the phone. "Did they leave a name?"

Bethany listened, brows furrowed like a plowed field. "Thank you for calling and letting me know. If you remember the name, please call me back. Okay?"

She listened a moment longer and then hung up. "You won't believe this."

"What?" He moved around behind the counter and stood beside her. He couldn't resist holding her shoulders. "Tell me."

"That was one of our best repeat clients, who's booked for our mid-July tour. He just received a phone call from another guest ranch offering to beat our price if they'd change their reservation. Ooh!" She slapped the counter then rubbed her hand. "That makes me so mad. Stealing customers is unethical."

"Well, now you know why you've had so many cancellations."

She gazed up at him with hurt in her dark brown eyes. "People out here watch out for one another. Who would do such a thing?"

Evan shook his head. "I'm sorry, but that's one thing I can't help you with since I don't know anyone around here. You'll have to discuss that with your dad."

Her eyes blurred with unshed tears. "Looks like I won't be starting my new job anytime soon."

Evan stuck his hands into his pockets, wishing he could pull her into his arms and comfort her. "Sounds like you're needed here."

"Yeah, it does." She sighed and swiped at a stream of tears running down her cheeks. "I just wish we knew who was causing all this trouble."

Evan snapped his fingers. "What if I registered under a different name and left my cell phone number? Now that I'm back here, it's working again."

"That might work. But how in the world could they be getting our reservation info?"

"Who has access to your cards?"

"Nobody. Just Dad and me."

"That's not totally true. The cards were here on the counter while you and I were eating. Anybody could have looked in the box while we were getting our food."

Her shoulders drooped. "You're right. Dad and I can't watch the desk constantly. We used to have a girl who worked here, but Dad. . ." She bit her lower lip as if she'd said too much.

He didn't want to push her to share more information than she was comfortable with. "So, basically anybody could have snooped in the box at a time when you and your dad were gone."

She nodded. "Yep. At least once all that information is on the computer, nobody will have access to it."

"Did you assign yourself a password?"

"No. I didn't think it was necessary with just Dad and me using it."

He laid his hand over hers. "It's necessary. That way you can leave and nobody else will be able to access it. I can help you set up a password if you don't know how."

"All right, let's do that and get you set up for another tour. What name do you want to use?" She opened her wooden file box and pulled out a blank card.

He tapped his finger against his lips and stared at the ceiling. "Daniel Lionheart. Group of four."

She lifted one eyebrow and looked at him as if he'd gone crazy. "Lionheart?"

He grinned. "Yeah, Daniel and the lions' den is one of my

favorite Bible stories. Can't you just imagine how scary it must have been to be thrown into a pit with a pride of hungry lions?"

She shivered. "I don't even want to think about it."

"I've always admired Daniel. He refused to bow to anyone except God, and it could have cost him his life. I want to be that bold in my walk with the Lord."

"I remember that story from when I was younger. I think I had a picture book that my mom read to me."

"Yeah, me, too."

She seemed to snap out of her melancholy moment. "Okay, Mr. Lionheart, what's your cell phone number?"

He rattled it off, wondering why she'd looked so sad for a moment. "I'll let you know ASAP if they call me."

"Okay, thanks. I think I'll call one of our regular clients and see if she and her friend would mind if I booked them, too. We might be more likely to hear something if there are two fake reservations."

"Good idea. Have you known those clients very long?"

She nodded. "You'd probably like them. Elsie and her friend Margaret—they're known as the Groovy Grannies—drive a hot pink semi and haul products."

"Seriously?"

Bethany smiled, warming his belly as much as the hot apple cobbler he'd just had for dessert. "Yeah, Elsie used to come here with her husband, but after he died, she brought her friend Margaret, who is also a widow. We love them both. Dad's been encouraging them to retire, but I can't imagine Elsie being happy staying in one place for any length of time." She sucked in a deep breath. "Listen, thanks for everything. It helps to have someone to talk things out with, and I'll tell Dad about your *marketing* ideas."

He chuckled at her emphasis on marketing. "I'm glad I could

help. I'd better head upstairs and get some work done." He walked away, wanting nothing more than to stay and spend more time with her. Too bad he was leaving so soon.

❧

Bethany watched Evan stride away. He wasn't as broad in the shoulders as the ranch hands who had done hard physical labor much of their lives, but he was tall and well built for a city boy. The elevator doors closed, but not before she saw him smile and wave. A warm sensation spiraled down her chest to her stomach.

Evan was thoughtful and logical, which was why he was probably very good at his job. He certainly was dedicated to his work—but not so much that he couldn't take breaks or come talk to her. He wasn't the nerd she'd first thought he was. She couldn't help grinning. "Well, he is a bit of a nerd."

"Who is?"

Bethany glanced up. "Maggie!"

"Hi. I was driving past the ranch and thought I'd stop in and see how things are going."

"Well, they've definitely been better. I'm so sorry Dad had to let you go."

Maggie shrugged. "Everyone's been hit by the bad economy. I'm working in town at Gertie's Café."

Bethany smiled. "I'm sure glad you found some other work. Are you interested in coming back here when things turn around?"

"When? Don't you mean 'if'?" Maggie leaned on the counter and propped her chin in her hands.

Bethany shook her head. "No, I mean 'when.' I have to believe things will get better."

"I suppose. Is your dad here? I wanted to say hi to him, too."

"He's gone on a tour, but you can hang around and talk to me if you want."

"Okay, I will. So, how do you like living in Denver?" Maggie tucked a strand of her black hair behind her ears. Her green eyes glistened with curiosity.

"I like it, I guess. I miss Dad and even have to say I miss the ranch at times."

Maggie laughed wryly. "I don't think I'd miss living in the sticks if I ever got away from here."

Bethany knew exactly how she felt, but her own desire to leave seemed to be fading. Maybe because her dad needed her or because of the ranch's problems. "Well, you'll be a senior next year, right? Got any plans for college?"

Maggie curled her lips. "As if my parents could afford it."

The girl's clothes looked new and of a high quality, not something a blue-collar worker like her father could afford. She was getting money from somewhere. "Well, maybe things will work out."

"Oh, hey. I've got a new boyfriend—Ryan Ogden. His family moved to Wyoming last year and started Ogden's Outfitters. It's a new guest ranch east of here on the old Scroggins land."

"Yeah, I heard someone talking about them, but I haven't met the owners yet." Bethany leaned forward. "Listen, I got a phone call just as I was finishing lunch and didn't have time for a pit stop. Would you mind hanging around a few minutes while I run to the restroom?"

"Sure. No problem."

Bethany logged on to the ranch's Web site. "Here, have a look at this while you're waiting. Let me know what you think."

Maggie slipped behind the counter. "Oh, wow! This is awesome. I love the animated wagon train."

Still listening eagerly to Maggie's excited responses, Bethany walked down the hall and into the restroom. She was glad that Maggie wasn't upset with them for laying her off. The girl had always been happy, and Bethany would have hated losing her friendship. Maybe they'd be able to rehire her when Bethany returned to Denver.

Back at the desk, she said good-bye to Maggie. She hated not being able to employ the cheerful teenager who loved people and had made a perfect desk clerk.

Bethany tapped on the keyboard, trying to set up a password. Finally, she sighed, giving up. That was another thing she needed Evan's help with. How would she have gotten her computer up and running without his assistance?

She thought about what he had said about Daniel refusing to bow down to anyone but God. She missed the closeness she felt to God as a child and young teen. If she hadn't walked away from Him, would the ranch be having the problems it was?

No, she couldn't believe that God worked that way. It was unfortunate that her father drained the bank account to pay off her college loans. Why had he done something so foolish when they could have made monthly payments?

Somehow, she'd pay back every penny. But not anytime soon. She didn't even draw a paycheck while working the ranch. Of course, there had always been plenty of money in the account to pay for the things she needed. She picked up the receiver and set it back down. She didn't want to do this, but she had no choice. Dad needed her. The ranch needed her. She punched in the phone number. Time to call her new boss and see if she could postpone her starting date.

twelve

"I sure hope I'm not making a big mistake here." Bethany climbed out of the Jeep and looked at Evan as he closed the passenger door.

"Trust me, you're not. Your guests will be thrilled that you've switched over to a wireless network. They'll be able to sit on their balconies or the lodge porch and check their e-mail or conduct business." He grinned, making her heart turn somersaults. "Welcome to the computer age."

"Well, I'm not there yet. We still have to find the right equipment, and that can be hard to do in these small Wyoming towns."

Evan met her in front of the Jeep and gazed around. "This town is a lot smaller than Laramie."

"Ya think?" Bethany blew a sarcastic laugh between her lips. "Try comparing it to Denver, where I've been living the past four years."

"It does kind of look like something out of a cowboy movie."

"Well, it's a tourist town. What else would you expect?" She tried to view the town from his eyes. No town in Wyoming even came close to what Denver had to offer, but that's what the locals loved about it. You could get close to nature here like you never could in a big city, and there was no quiet like that of the mountain valleys. She shook her head. She was getting nostalgic in her old age.

"Point the way, tour guide."

"Yes, sir, city slicker." Bethany smiled and pointed. "It's that store across the street."

They walked to the corner and waited for the light to change. The streets were crowded with vacationers strolling along, carrying packages, and dodging in and out of stores.

A car started to turn left in front of a pickup. Tires screeched, and the truck driver laid on his horn. Bethany jumped and stepped closer to Evan. She liked the amenities a town had to offer, but she hated traffic and congestion. In truth, she *was* a country girl at heart.

The light turned green. Evan grabbed her hand as if it was a common occurrence and tugged her forward in the crosswalk. She liked the feel of her hand in his bigger one. It felt solid and strong. She doubted he even realized what he'd done, and she shouldn't enjoy feeling as if she belonged to him, but for this one moment, she would.

He opened the door, allowing her to enter first. His hand rested lightly on her lower back as he looked around the store. He pointed in the air. "Over there."

Evan guided her toward the back of the store where the wireless routers were located. As he studied the few available, she watched him. He looked like a wide-eyed child riding his first horse, minus the fear element.

"Okay." He picked up a box. "I recommend this one. Do you want the Muskrat Lodge to also be wireless?"

She hadn't considered that yet, but the cost of the router wasn't as much as she'd expected, and they'd be offering wireless Internet access to more of their guests. "How many routers would you need if we did the main lodge and Muskrat?"

"Two, probably. What about the cabins?"

She thought for a moment then shook her head. "I think we should leave those as they are for people who are coming to get away from the rat race."

"Okay, then two should be enough." He grabbed a package of cables. "We can hook the router for the main lodge to your new computer, but we'll need to find a closet or utility room for the one at Muskrat Lodge."

They selected a new printer and then checked out. She could almost imagine them as a married couple in town to do their shopping for the week. She probably shouldn't have spent the money for the routers, but Evan was right—they needed to offer top-of-the-line service to be competitive with other outfitters. Besides, who knew how much she would have had to pay if she'd hired someone to do the work? Evan seemed to enjoy helping her with her computer woes. Was she taking advantage of him?

Suddenly he stopped in the middle of the sidewalk, his nose tilted in the air. Tourists gawked and made a wide clearing around him. He looked one way then another. His sky blue eyes sparked. "Pizza. I smell pizza."

Bethany couldn't help giggling. He was like a big kid. He tucked the sack of computer supplies under his right arm and looped his left arm through hers.

"C'mon. I'm buying lunch. Two weeks is too long for a man to live without pizza."

"You don't have to buy lunch. We can eat at the ranch," she protested but couldn't help the pleasant feeling swelling inside her. This was almost like a date. An impromptu date.

They took a seat in a booth, and Evan looked at her. "What's your pleasure, ma'am?"

"Hamburger."

"Just hamburger? Where's your sense of adventure?"

"Oh, I have all the adventure I can handle, thank you. But maybe I will get something different today." She tapped her finger on her lips. "Hamburger with black olives."

Evan grinned. "I like a woman who's not afraid to step out and take a chance."

A skinny young man with big ears and teeth stopped at

their table. "You guys ready to order?"

"Give us a large thick crust. Half supreme and half hamburger with black olives. I'll take a Coke, and the lady wants. . ." He lifted his brows.

"Iced tea." The waiter nodded and walked away as Bethany plucked two packages of sugar from a little dish near the salt shaker. "So, I guess you'll be happy to get back home."

"Yeah, all this fresh air is clogging my sinuses."

She shook her head.

"Seriously, though. There are things I will miss about this place. I can't believe I've lived my whole life in Wyoming and never visited the mountains before. My parents never traveled much, and I've been busy working." He tapped his fingertips on the table as if he were typing on his keyboard.

Bethany couldn't help wondering if she was one of the things he'd miss. How had she gone from crowning him the greenest among the greenhorns to hating to see him leave? His gaze lifted from the table and collided with hers. For a moment she couldn't breathe at the intensity of his stare.

"I'll miss *you*, Bethany."

He glanced away, as if fearing her rejection. She ought to nip things in the bud, but the truth was, she'd miss him, too. He'd sneaked in under her radar and stolen a piece of her heart. But like all the others she'd befriended or cared about, he'd be leaving—soon. Still, she couldn't lie to him. "I'll miss you, too."

His hopeful gaze swerved back to hers. His lips tilted upward, and he slid his hand across the table. Hers move forward to meet his, as if it had a mind of its own. He clutched it tight. "So. . .what are we going to do about this?"

She shrugged and pulled her hand back. "Nothing. You'll go back to your world, as I will."

Scowling, he repeatedly flicked the edge of his napkin with his index finger, and she thought he'd drop the subject. The waiter delivered their drinks, and Evan captured her gaze again. He sighed. "I won't lie to you. I don't have much experience with women. I dated a few times, but most girls prefer jocks to geeks. I don't want things to end like this. At least we can e-mail each other and stay friends."

"Yeah, sure. We can do that." She knew how e-mailing worked. The first week or two there would be a ton of messages, but as the weeks drew on, there'd be fewer and fewer. Maybe it was better to play along, knowing how things would eventually end. That way he'd be hurt less than if she just dropped him now. She had to protect her heart. No one else could do that job.

ðə

Their pizza arrived, and they ate quickly, talking little.

He'd pushed too hard, and now she was pulling back. But he didn't have much time left.

Maybe this was God's way of telling him that she wasn't the woman for him. A Christian shouldn't be yoked with an unbeliever—he knew that—but for a short time he'd allowed himself to run on emotions instead of logical thinking.

Bethany flicked her hair out of her face, and he longed to touch it, to see if it was as soft as it looked.

Stop it, Parker. How could he lose his heart so fast, and to a country girl who didn't want to live in the country? He straightened. If she didn't want the country, would she consider living in Laramie? It wasn't Denver, but maybe it could be a nice compromise. Nah, he'd better just be happy that she agreed to be friends.

Bethany shoved back her plate and finished her drink. Evan jumped up. "Ready to go?"

She flinched, as if surprised by his sudden movement. Nodding, she grabbed her purse.

He walked toward the checkout register, ready to get back to the ranch and away from her. He'd been a fool to bare his heart when he knew things could never work out. What was he thinking?

He'd seen what happened in Erin's life when a Christian married an unbeliever. Sure, things had been bearable for a while, but in the end, Clint had walked away from his family, leaving behind a debris trail as wide as an EF-5 tornado and a hurting wife and children. Evan had been the one to step in and clean up that mess, and he wasn't about to make the same mistake.

He'd been stupid to think things could work out between him and Bethany, to even consider a relationship with a woman who wasn't sold out to God. He just had to face reality and make his heart stop aching.

thirteen

Bethany tapped her finger on the phone receiver. *Should I call him or not?*

She needed Evan's help with another computer problem but hated calling him after he'd all but given her the cold shoulder then stayed in his room after they'd returned from town yesterday. He hadn't even come down for dinner or this morning's breakfast.

She couldn't exactly blame him.

The elevator doors opened, and Bethany's heart jolted. She was half disappointed and half relieved when Taylor got off instead of Evan. The teen waved and stopped at the counter. Almost two weeks in the sun had tanned her skin to a golden brown, highlighting her blue eyes. She was a pretty girl who would grow into a beautiful woman as long as she kept her attitude in check.

"Hey, Miss Schaffer."

Bethany smiled. "Looking for Cheryl again?"

Taylor nodded and glanced out the front window as if searching for her friend. A black SUV pulled into one of the parking spaces, leaving a cloud of dust trailing behind it.

"Um...I probably shouldn't say anything..." Taylor glanced up, an intensity in her eyes. She nibbled on her lower lip, revealing front teeth with the tiniest of gaps. "My uncle may be a geek, but he's a really nice guy. I don't know what we would have done after my dad left without Uncle Evan's help." She looked back at Bethany. "He doesn't have a lot of experience with women. I hope you'll give him a break. He really likes you."

Bethany felt as if her mom had just given her a well-deserved lecture. "I like him, too, but I don't want to lead him on. You guys are leaving, and so am I. Soon. There's no future for us together."

Taylor raised her gaze, probably up to the moose head on the wall behind Bethany. "Never say never. God can do amazing things. Just give Uncle Evan a chance, will you?"

An older couple walked up the front stairs, and the man held the door open for his female companion, probably his wife. In that split second, Bethany wondered what it would be like to grow old with Evan.

Taylor peeked over her shoulder then flashed a tight-lipped smile. "I probably shouldn't have said anything, but I hate to see my uncle looking sad. He does so much for others that he deserves some happiness of his own."

Bethany watched the teen walk toward the dining hall. *How had the girl changed from Miss Attitude to Wise Sage so quickly?*

She shook her head, putting Evan and Taylor out of her mind as she registered the new guests. Five minutes later she escorted them to their room on the same floor as Evan's. "I hope you have an enjoyable stay here at Moose Valley Ranch. Please let me know if you have questions or if there's anything I can assist you with."

"Thank you, miss." The man closed the door to the room.

As Bethany walked past Evan's door, her steps slowed. She ought to keep walking. She could figure out the problem herself, but it might take hours. Sighing, she lifted her hand and knocked.

The door handle jiggled, and then Evan stood before her, a slight scowl wrinkling his forehead. His hair was messed up, as if he'd been running his hands through it. His eyes looked tired and red, as if he hadn't slept the night before.

Was she responsible for his rumpled state? Hadn't she only

been protecting her own heart? It pained her to think she might have hurt him. She ducked her head.

He reached out, lifting her chin with his index finger. "Hey."

Every fiber of her body seemed happy to be in his presence again. She cleared her throat. "I was, uh. . ."

Evan's brows lifted.

"I was wondering if I could buy you a pop."

His eyes sparked; then wariness descended, stealing away her hope that he would agree. "Why?"

Pulling away from his stern gaze, she noticed a frayed edge of carpet at the door's threshold. *Better let Dad know about that before it gets worse.*

She took a strengthening breath. The discomfort between them was her fault because she had tried to distance herself from him. Could they actually be friends and leave it at that?

Bethany shrugged. She could really use a good friend. She summoned a smile to her face. "I thought maybe you'd need a caffeine fix about now. . .and I could use some help on the computer."

He faked a brief laugh. "Ah, so the truth comes out." He rubbed the back of his neck. "I guess I could use a break. Just let me save my current work."

She watched him walk over to the coffee table where his laptop sat. He made a couple of swift hand movements and stood. Beside the couch on the end table was a tray of dirty dishes. "Mind if I grab that tray and take it downstairs?"

"I'll get it." He snatched up the tray and held it so high she couldn't reach it, even standing on tiptoes.

"You're the guest. I should be carrying that."

He pulled his door shut. "Maybe, but I was the one who ate the food."

Bethany sighed and trotted down the stairs with Evan beside her. Their being together felt right somehow. Like wearing matching shoes or hitching the correct team of horses to a wagon. She was in dangerous territory, allowing her thoughts to travel along such lines.

At the counter, Evan lowered the tray and she grabbed for it. He raised it over her head again, sidestepped around her, and grinned. "How about you unlock the store, and I'll return this to the kitchen?"

"Fine." She conceded her loss with a smile of her own. She liked this playful side of Evan Parker. In the store she grabbed two cans of pop and a bag of chips. She wrote a note that she'd taken them so she could deduct the items from their inventory later, then locked the door. Evan joined her at the counter.

"So. . .what seems to be the problem this time?"

She told him and stood beside him, watching the master at work. She was no dummy concerning computers, but he seemed to know them inside and out. It amazed her how he could fix something in five or ten minutes that took her hours, if she could fix it at all. Leaning toward the monitor to get a better look, her arm touched his. He'd rolled up his sleeve, and this arm was free of spots. The warmth of his skin soaked into hers and made her hands tingle. He seemed oblivious but shifted his feet and leaned a bit closer, all the while jiggling the mouse and working the keyboard. His milk chocolate hair hung across his forehead, and his lips moved as if helping him.

The doors opened, and her father strode in. Bethany hopped back a half step, putting distance between her and Evan. He glanced sideways and grinned. The rascal had been aware of her nearness all along if she wasn't mistaken.

"What are you doing back, Dad? There haven't been any more problems, have there?"

He shook his head. "Nope. Jenny's running low on sugar and some other stuff, so I made the run back here. Got another problem with that crazy computer?" Her dad barely glanced at them as he walked around the counter and into the office. "Don't know how you expect *me* to run that thing when you can't even get it working. I'm going to have to build a house for Evan so he can stick around and help keep that computer working."

She wasn't sure if her dad was just mumbling to himself or complaining loud enough for them to hear on purpose. Teaching him to run the computer was a big concern. He was a skilled man, but with horses, cattle, and ranch equipment, not electronics. Maybe she ought to figure out a way to rehire Maggie. Having the teen work the counter as she had last summer would free Bethany to do other jobs.

Something that sounded like a foghorn blasted outside. Evan jerked his head up and stared out the front window at the same time Bethany did. What in the world? A huge pink RV stopped along the back edge of the parking lot.

"Talk about Pepto-Bismol. I can honestly say I've never seen anything quite like that." Evan stared openly at the huge vehicle.

Bethany rounded the counter and squinted at the lettering on the side of the motor home. In fancy gold script, she read, THE GROOVY GRANNIES. "Oh my goodness! Dad! Elsie and Margaret are here—and they're not in their semitruck."

"Two grandmas drive that thing?" Evan's surprised expression made her giggle.

Her dad came out of the office and strode toward the door. "What do you mean they're not in their semi?"

"Well. . .look!"

He muttered under his breath. "I tried to talk them into selling that pink semi last time they was here, but I never expected them to buy something as hideous as that."

She hugged him. "Be nice, Dad. They're entitled to live their lives the way they want."

Bethany dashed out the door and jogged down the steps.

Elsie had traveled the country hauling freight the past few years with her friend Margaret even though both of the women's families had tried hard to get them to retire. It looked as if they finally had.

"Howdy!" Elsie climbed out of the RV and waved, her silver hair sparkling in the sunlight. Wearing leather boots, a pink tank top, and shorts, she stepped to the ground. She enveloped Bethany in a bear hug. "My, just look at you. You're so lovely."

"And look at you. You're retired." She pushed back to see Elsie's wrinkled face. "You are retired, right?"

Elsie nodded as Margaret, wearing a lavender sweat suit and black sunglasses with shiny sequins along the top, rounded the front of the RV. "That's right. We are officially retired."

"Then what's this contraption?" Bethany's father waved his big hand in the air.

Elsie shoved her fists to her slim waist. "What did you expect, Rob? That we were just going to retire in some old folks' home?"

Bethany grinned. "I don't think he ever expected you to retire at all. So, what brings you out here?"

"We came for our wagon tour."

Bethany glanced at her dad. "But that was just a test registration to see if anyone would call and offer you a better deal at some other ranch. That hasn't happened, has it?"

It was Margaret's turn to get her feathers ruffled. "Well, if they did, we'd have given them what for. Imagine stealing your customers. Why that's unethical."

Bethany looped her arm through Elsie's and tugged her toward the lodge. "Still, I never meant that you actually had to go on the tour."

"We want to. We have all the time in the world now."

Her dad offered his arm to Margaret, and the two followed them inside. "Let's all go get something cool to drink. My treat."

"You're so generous, Rob," Elsie joked and patted Bethany's arm. "I thought you were starting a new job in Denver, dear."

Bethany darted a glance at her father and noticed his lips tighten. "We can talk about all that later. I want to hear what you've been doing."

They marched inside, but as Bethany turned toward the dining hall, Elsie tugged her in the other direction, toward the counter.

"My, my. I'd say that young man is quite an improvement over that young tart you had working here before."

Evan's vivid blue eyes widened as he looked up from the monitor.

"Whew! And look at those eyes. Just like Paul Newman's." Elsie turned to Bethany and whispered, "I do hope you're planning on keeping him."

Her cheeks felt as if they'd been torched. "He doesn't work here, Elsie. Evan's a guest who's helping me get the new computer system up and running."

Elsie turned loose of her arm and walked up to the counter. "Come along, young man. We're taking refreshment in the dining hall."

Evan's questioning gaze rushed to Bethany's. She didn't mind him joining them and nodded toward the dining hall. He looked down and made a few quick taps on the keyboard then offered one arm to Elsie and carried his pop can in the other. "I already have a drink, but I'd enjoy the company."

Margaret took Evan's other arm. "You can't have him all to yourself, Els."

Bethany suppressed a grin. Evan looked bewildered but smiled down at the two older women and led them into the dining hall as if he were escorting royalty.

Over tea and pie, they caught up on all that had been going on at the ranch. Elsie pushed back her empty plate. "I don't like that all these strange things have been happening."

"Maybe the prankster has gotten tired. You haven't had any problems here while I was gone, have you?" Bethany's father looked across the table at her, and she shook her head.

"Nope, nothing but some cancellations."

"Good, maybe that's over with." Elsie smiled at Evan as he took a swallow of pop. "Are you married, young man?"

Bethany stifled a gasp as Evan worked hard not to spew his drink. He pounded his chest and coughed. "Uh. . .no, ma'am."

Elsie winked at Bethany, and Margaret smiled as if she'd won the lottery. Bethany shoved back her chair and stood. "Don't you think we should get back to work, Evan?"

He nodded and stood. "Nice to meet you both."

If Bethany hadn't been as anxious to leave as he was, she might have laughed at his hasty escape.

❧

Evan leaned against the corral and watched Taylor lead a golden horse out of the barn. She'd called it a palo-something. She waved, warming his heart. If nothing else, this trip had brought them closer together. He prayed that when they returned home she wouldn't cop an attitude like before.

The setting sun sent lances of light into the pink and orange clouds, creating a view that took his breath away. Only the almighty God could have created such a magnificent sight. He forced his gaze away so that he could concentrate on Taylor.

"Watch me, Uncle Evan." She nudged her horse in the side, and it jolted into a trot. Taylor bounced up and down.

He clenched the railing, afraid that at any moment she'd fall to the ground and he'd have to call Erin to explain how Taylor had broken her arm. He climbed up on the bottom rail and was ready to yell at her to stop when the horse broke into a smooth lope that settled Taylor into the saddle.

Someone slapped him on the shoulder, and he jumped. "Easy, city boy; she's doing fine."

He lowered himself to the ground and glanced at Bethany before turning back to watch Taylor. "Tell that to my heart."

She chuckled.

Near the barn door, Cheryl bounced up and down. "Yee-haw! Ride 'em, cowgirl."

Taylor's megawatt grin could have lit up the whole city of Laramie.

Bethany climbed onto the fence and placed a hand on her brow to shield her eyes from the sun as Taylor rode around the corral. "She's gotten quite good at riding in a short time. You might want to think about finding a place for her to ride when you go home."

He tightened his grip on the wooden rail. He didn't want to think of leaving in two days. Of never seeing Bethany again—but she'd made her position clear. She would be his friend, but she wasn't willing to risk her heart on a computer geek from the city. His pride took a nosedive, but it wasn't the first time.

"Has Taylor talked to you about tonight?"

His niece made several circles around the corral then rode the horse back toward the barn. Cheryl walked out and took the reins while Taylor slid off. Evan turned to face Bethany. The sky was darkening, but he could still see her well in the twilight. "What about tonight?"

She pursed her lips then looked up. "I guess it's no secret that Taylor and Cheryl have become good friends. Polly asked me earlier if you might consider letting Taylor spend the night with Cheryl."

Evan's gut tightened. Should he let his niece stay with people they barely knew? Sure, they seemed like decent folk, but what would Erin do?

Bethany must have sensed his concern, because she laid her hand on his arm, warming it through his sleeve. "I've known Shep and Polly Wilkes most of my life, and I can vouch for them. They're good folk. Taylor will be fine with them."

Cheryl handed the horse off to her dad, and the two girls raced toward him, their eyes lit up as they climbed over the corral fence.

"Did you ask him?" Cheryl directed her question to Bethany. She nodded.

"You'll have to ask your mother." He didn't mind passing the buck to stay out of trouble.

Taylor grinned. "I already did, and she said I could if you thought it was okay."

He was cornered. He'd met Shep Wilkes once and liked the man, but the bottom line was that he trusted Bethany's judgment. Evan nodded, and the girls squealed and high-fived each other.

"Let's go pack your stuff," Cheryl said, bouncing up and down.

Both girls took off running, but Taylor slid to a halt and jogged back. She wrapped her arms around Evan's waist. "Thanks!"

Before he could return her hug, she was gone.

"You did the right thing. They'll have a blast." Bethany smiled. "Cheryl gets lonely living here. Trust me, I know."

Something about the melancholy in her voice touched a spot deep within him, and he longed for her to know God more closely—to know Him as the Friend who was always there. Who would never desert her. Maybe she could never be his, but if he could introduce her to his Savior, he wouldn't worry about her so much once he was gone. He stared out at the darkening sky. "Would a country gal be interested in taking a walk with a city boy?"

She cocked her head. A smile danced on her lips. "Why not? Dad's gone back to the campsite, so there's nobody waiting for me."

He stuck out his arm, and she looped hers through it. "Which way?"

She tugged him toward the barn. "There's a hill we can climb and see the sunset better."

They walked in silence, and when the climbing became more difficult, she let go of his arm but he captured her hand. Friends could hold hands, right?

Her skin was soft and warm, and she didn't pull away. As they topped the steep hill, the sky brightened a bit. The sun had already disappeared behind the mountains, but the distant horizon glowed like a pinkish-orange neon rope light. "It's beautiful."

"Yeah. I haven't been out here in a long while." She stood quietly for a few minutes then cleared her throat. "I, uh, have something to ask you."

"Yeah?" He turned to face her.

"Dad and I were wondering if you might be willing to stay on a few more days to help make sure the computer is up and running. We can't pay you anything, but you could keep the suite and we'd feed you. He also wanted me to tell you that we'd like you to come back with your sister and her kids and take another wagon tour. You've been such a big help that we wanted to do something for you." The words seemed to rush out of her, as if she were afraid to voice them.

Evan shook his head and grinned. "No thanks on the tour, at least for me."

He considered her offer to stay longer. He was making excellent progress on his project now that he was feeling better, and with Internet service, he'd been able to do several video conferences with his team. As far as he knew, Taylor didn't have anything that she had to do once they returned home, but he should probably call Erin to make sure.

"It's okay if you can't. Dad wanted me to ask you."

His excitement at spending more time with Bethany spiraled down like a marble on a twisting slide. "Your dad—or you?"

"Both of us." She shrugged in the waning light. To her right, the lodge and buildings glowed as lights popped on. "Okay, it was my idea, but Dad is in full agreement."

Evan smiled then. "I'd like that, but I do need to check with Erin."

She nodded and turned back toward the mountains. Feeling brave, Evan wrapped his arm loosely around Bethany's shoulders. She glanced up at him then focused back on the sunset.

"God sure made some beautiful sights," he said. "I can't believe I've lived my whole life in Wyoming and never been here before."

"It's like any other place. When you live here and have seen it so often, you take it for granted. I know I do at times."

"Yeah, just like people take God for granted."

She stiffened but after a moment relaxed. "I was close to Him as a child, but after Mom died and Dad wouldn't take me to church, I drifted away."

"It's never too late to make things right with God." He tightened his grip on her shoulders.

She sighed loudly. "I don't know how to."

"All you have to do is pray. Acknowledge your need for God and believe that Jesus died for your sins. God is always waiting for you to come to Him."

She shrugged. "You make it sound so easy."

Evan turned to face her again and rested his wrists on her shoulders. "It is easy. All you have to do is express your need for God and ask Him to come into your heart."

"Seriously?"

"Yep." With the sky nearly black, Evan could barely see Bethany's face. "All you have to do is ask."

She sniffled. "I've been angry with God for so long. I still don't understand why He had to take my mother away when I needed her so much."

Evan stroked her hair, wanting to comfort her. "People get sick. They have accidents. But God can give us the strength we need to make it through those rough times."

"I want to make things right with God." She ducked her head and leaned it against his chest. "Will you help me, Evan?"

His heart took off like a racehorse from a starting gate. "I'd love to."

He said the words, and she repeated them after him, asking God to forgive her sins and to come into her heart anew.

Bethany looped her arms around his waist, and Evan couldn't resist hugging her back. "Now you never have to be alone. God will be your Friend."

"Yeah. That's pretty cool."

He could feel her tears dampening his shirt. She may not be his, but she would always be the Lord's.

After a few minutes, Bethany loosened her grip and stepped back. Reluctantly, he let her go. She lifted up on her tiptoes and placed a brief kiss on his lips. Evan felt his eyes widen in the dark and longed to keep her from leaving, to hold her tight and let her know the depth of his feelings. But now wasn't the time.

"Thank you. I will always appreciate how you brought me back to the Lord."

They walked down the hill. Evan knew he should be thrilled that she'd reconciled with God—and he was. But he wanted more. He wanted her in his life.

Maybe staying longer wasn't such a good idea, after all.

fourteen

"You're sooo lucky. I wish I was staying longer." Misty Chamberlain hugged Taylor before climbing into the school van.

Evan watched his niece saying good-bye to all her friends, glad that he had decided to stay on a few more days. He opened his laptop, ready to do some work on the lodge porch while enjoying the warm sunshine.

Sarah James walked out of the lodge with another girl, carrying a Coke and a sack of chips. "I can't wait to get home and eat junk food again and watch TV."

A boy carrying a duffel bag jogged down the steps past her. "You would, you couch potato."

Sarah scowled and stuck out her tongue at him, then walked down the stairs. Chuckles sounded all around as two boys tossed gear into the van.

It was no wonder Taylor struggled with attitude problems when she was around these kids all the time at school. Evan wished he could afford to send his niece and nephew to a Christian school. He typed in his password.

Taylor waved good-bye to her friends and teacher, then walked toward the corral where Cheryl sat on the top railing waiting for her. His niece had been ecstatic when Evan asked if she wanted to stay a few more days. He wasn't quite so thrilled, but after praying, he felt it was what God wanted him to do. Maybe things could still work out between him and Bethany—or maybe the Lord wanted him around to help strengthen her new walk with God before he left.

He sighed and tapped on his keyboard. The van driver

honked as the tires crackled on the gravel and pulled away, leaving behind a trail of dust. Fortunately, the dirt cloud floated away from him instead of toward him.

Staring out at the mountains glistening in the morning sun, he heaved a sigh. He just wasn't in the mood to work today. Maybe he could go riding with Taylor and Cheryl, not that the teens would want a greenhorn uncle tagging along. If he had a swimsuit, he could enjoy the pool. With the school group gone and a new group of guests already on the second day of a new wagon tour, there were few people about the ranch.

He stood and stretched. What he needed was a jog. He'd been idle too long after being sick, and his muscles were tight and stiff. A cloud of dust still lingered over the valley the van had just driven through. If he jogged down the road, would the cows bother him?

Shaking his head, he closed his laptop. Bethany would certainly tease him if she thought he was apprehensive of cows. Not cows exactly, but more the unknown. His mood soured, and he realized this was just another way they were incompatible.

He picked up his laptop and headed toward the front door.

Bethany nearly knocked him down on her way out. Her eyes were wild with worry, and she stared past the barn, not even noticing he was there.

"What's wrong?" He grabbed her arm until she looked at him.

Her gaze took a moment to register his presence. "Dad's been hurt."

"How?"

She turned away, keeping her vigil again. "Steve's bringing him in. He just called and said Dad was unconscious."

Evan's heart lurched.

"Jim hitched up the teams this morning, but afterward, someone cut the traces and several other parts of the harness on Dad's wagon. When Dad ordered his team to go, the horses walked forward, but the wagon didn't move. Dad was jerked off the wagon seat. . . ."

She clutched his arm, tears in her eyes. "Oh, Evan. I can't lose him. He's all I've got."

Evan set his computer back on the table and held her shoulders. "He's not all you have. You've got God now—and you've got me."

Leaning against his chest, she sobbed. Evan was stunned to see this woman who was normally so in control of her feelings falling apart. He held her until she pulled away and looked again toward the wagon trail.

"Listen, sweetheart. I'm going to run my laptop up to my room. Why don't you get your keys and purse? That way we can take your dad to the hospital as soon as he arrives." Evan picked up his computer. "There is a hospital in town, right?"

Bethany nodded then spun around. "No, but there's a clinic."

"All right. I'll run upstairs. Could you call Shep and see if he'd keep an eye on the girls? I don't know his number."

"Yeah." She raced past him and through the front door, seeming happy to have something to do.

Evan glanced toward the trail. No sign of the Jeep yet. He ran up the stairs, taking two at a time. "Please, Father. Let Rob be okay. Bethany needs him. Don't take him from her."

❧

"I'm not going to no doctor." Bethany's dad slid forward from the back of the Jeep where he'd been lying down and sat on the tailgate. He listed to the left, and she reached out to steady him. He swatted her hand away, and with one of Jenny's towels from the cookhouse, he swiped at the blood dripping down his temple. He stood, wobbled, and sat back down. Steve stood beside the Jeep scowling.

Her heart ached. Her father's jaw was swollen, and blood

seeped from a goose egg on his forehead. He held his left arm close to his chest and weaved sideways as he tried to stand again.

"I'm not taking no for an answer. Get in my Jeep, Dad."

She gently reached under his right arm and helped him to straighten as he mumbled something about her being bossy. Steve stayed close to Rob's side and stood ready to assist if needed, but with her dad's confounded pride, she should count her blessings that he was allowing her to help him at all.

Evan ran out the front doors with something in his hands, and Bethany's nerves settled a measure just having him near.

"Polly cornered me and sent an ice bag. How is he?"

"He's fine," her father growled.

The fact that he let her put him in her Jeep instead of going into the lodge proved that he wasn't as well as he claimed. Her heart stumbled at that thought. He leaned his head back, and she buckled his seat belt and closed the door. Evan handed her the ice pack, and she passed it to her dad through the window. "Keep this on your forehead."

He mumbled something else but did as he was told.

She motioned Steve to the front of the vehicle. "How long was he unconscious?"

The ranch hand shook his head. "Hard to say, because I was driving and his wagon was in the back. He was out from the time he fell until after we got him in the Jeep and I was well on my way back. Twenty minutes maybe."

Bethany winced. "That's a long time."

Evan took her hand and squeezed it. "We'd better get going before your dad changes his mind."

She nodded. "Anything else I need to know?"

Steve shrugged. "The wagon was hitched up properly. I know because I did it myself." He lifted off his hat and scratched the back of his head. "I just don't see how anyone could have gotten in and cut the harnesses without any of us noticing."

Bethany sighed. "You guys be careful. It's obvious that someone is sabotaging our trips and stealing our customers. I just wish we could find out who it is before a guest gets hurt and we find ourselves facing a lawsuit."

Evan took her shoulders and propelled her toward the driver's seat. "Don't worry about that right now. Just get in and drive."

Steve lifted his brows, and she knew he wondered why this guest she'd poked fun at was ordering her around. She obeyed and climbed into the Jeep, more to avoid Steve and his questions than anything else. Evan crawled in the backseat and closed the door.

She started the engine, backed out, then stepped on the gas. The Jeep shot forward, and her dad moaned. Feeling guilty for causing him pain, she slowed down. *Please, God, he has to be okay. I'll even come back and stay at the ranch if that's what it takes. Just let Dad be all right. I need him, God.*

An hour and a half later, Bethany paced the waiting room of the small clinic. She gulped down the last of her coffee, crumpled the paper cup, and tossed it at the trash can. She missed. "What's taking so long?"

Evan stood and stretched, then put the cup in the trash. "They're probably just being thorough."

She heard a shuffling noise and watched the doorway. Dr. Franklin ambled in, drying his hands on some paper towels. He caught her eye and smiled. "He's going to be fine."

She strode across the room toward him. "How bad is it?"

The doctor nodded at Evan as he joined her, his shoulder touching hers. "He has those cuts on his head and a concussion. He also broke his wrist in the fall."

"Oh," she gasped, and Evan wrapped his arm around her shoulders. She leaned her weight into his side. "Dad is so independent. How will he ever tend to himself with a broken wrist?"

"Well, you've answered your own question, young lady. Rob comes from tough stock. He's independent and will manage, although I suspect he may need your help with some things for a while."

"I know. I'm just overly worried."

"I gave him something for the pain, and it will make him sleep for a while. Why don't you two go grab something to eat, and maybe you could show this young man some of our town."

"There's not that much to see."

The doctor lifted his brows. "People sure pay a load of money to come here."

She ducked her head and studied the cracked tile at her feet. "Yeah, I know."

Evan squeezed her shoulders. "I could use some lunch. I think we'll take your advice, Doc, since Rob will be sleeping."

Bethany wanted to argue, but the fight seemed to have oozed out of her.

The doctor looked at Evan. "You're sure looking better than the last time I saw you. How are you doing? Everything healing all right?"

Evan nodded. "Yes, that medicine you prescribed sure did the trick. I was better in a few days."

"Good. You're fortunate. Chicken pox in adults can been severe and cause shingles." He offered a tired smile. "Well, I'd better get back to my patient."

Bethany allowed Evan to guide her out of the empty waiting room, past the check-in desk where a nurse was busy working on charts, and outside. The sun made her squint after being inside for so long. The hum of cars greeted her as they passed on the street. She heard someone honk and yell. Scents from a nearby café made her stomach gurgle, and she glanced at her watch, surprised that they had missed lunch. She hadn't even noticed. Evan's arm slid off her shoulders.

"So, what will it be?"

She shrugged. "I don't care. Anything is fine."

"Are you okay?"

When she looked up, he ran his finger down her cheek. She was surprised that it had a rough feel to it and wasn't as soft as she'd expected. Could a guy get calluses from typing so much? She smiled.

"What?"

"Nothing. That café across the street has pretty good food—unless you'd rather have pizza again."

"Whatever. You choose." He tucked a strand of windblown hair behind her ear and rested his hand on her cheek.

Her heart swelled with affection for him. He was a good, caring man. Why couldn't their lives be more similar?

His eyes darkened, and she wondered if he would kiss her. Instead, he pulled her into his arms and held her tight. She buried her face against his clean shirt and smelled his spicy aftershave. He was warm and solid. His hand crushed her head against him, and he kissed her hair. Bethany clung to him, wishing she could stay forever in the shelter of his arms without worry or concern.

Evan's phone chirped. He loosened his grip with one arm and reached into his pocket. "H'lo."

She could hear the hum of someone talking but couldn't tell what they were saying. Evan stiffened.

"I might be," he said. He gripped her shoulder and pushed her back. "Tell me more."

He motioned for her to get a pen and paper.

"Yeah, that is a much better deal. What did you say the name of your place was? Ogden Outfitters?" Bethany felt as if she were falling face-first off a cliff. He must be talking to the competing guest ranch. Why did that name sound familiar?

"Can I think about it and call you back?"

The voice on the phone buzzed.

"I understand. I realize you can't give everyone such a great deal. Let me talk to my friends and see if they'll agree to make the change to your ranch. I'll call back in a few hours. What's your phone number?"

He waved at the paper and quoted a number. She wrote it down along with the ranch name.

Evan hung up and grinned. "We got 'em."

"How in the world did they get your number?"

He shrugged. "Obviously, someone went through your file box again."

Bethany pursed her lips and forced her feet to move. "C'mon. Let's get lunch. I want to be there when Dad wakes up."

Evan took her hand, and as if they'd decided together, they both walked toward the café that had a two-foot hamburger painted on the window in vivid colors. Something was nagging at her memory. Where had she heard that name before?

Suddenly she halted and pulled Evan around to face her. The wind whipped at his nut brown hair, making it even more unruly than normal. She clutched his forearm. "Now I remember. Maggie, the desk clerk Dad laid off last month, stopped by this week to say hi. She said she was dating a guy whose father owned Ogden Outfitters, a neighboring guest ranch that's only been in business a short while. That's why the name sounded so familiar."

Evan scowled. "How well do you know this Maggie?"

Bethany waved her hand in the air. "Oh, she's a sweet girl from town who worked for us last summer. She wouldn't do anything to hurt us."

Evan's brows lifted. "Your dad laid her off, and she's dating the son of your newest competitor. Talk about motive."

She opened her mouth, but her gut clenched with disbelief. Surely Maggie couldn't be involved. Bethany gasped and lifted her hand to her mouth, a feeling of betrayal slicing through her. "I left Maggie alone at the counter the day she visited so I could—uh. . .never mind." She looked up at Evan, shock fogging her brain. "I left her at the counter, Evan."

fifteen

"I think we ought to call the sheriff rather than handle this ourselves." Evan held on to the door frame as Bethany drove her Jeep like a maniac. The wind whipped his shirt like a flag, and grit coated his teeth.

"We handle things ourselves out here."

"I don't believe that for a minute. These people could be dangerous. Look at all the pranks they've pulled. Obviously, they don't care if they hurt people." The engine roared as she gunned it up a steep hill. A sign indicated a right turn onto Ogden land.

She careened around the corner, barely slowing down. Evan flung out his foot as if to hit the brake and used his left hand to brace himself against the dash.

Bethany peeked at him and smiled. "You're such a city boy. Don't you enjoy a drive in the country?"

"Not when I feel like I'm riding in an ambulance minus the tires. All that's missing is the siren." He shook his head. "Remind me not to ride with you when you're upset."

Ten minutes later, she pulled into a crowded parking lot. White buildings and cottages with green roofs dotted the hillside. A huge barn sat off to the side and down a hill with a creek running not far from it. A trio of rafts floated down the creek with several people in each one. The view of the mountains was spectacular but farther away than the view from Moose Valley.

"Looks like business is good here," he said.

Bethany sniffed a laugh. "Yeah, it ought to be, the way

they've been stealing customers."

Two long-legged cowboys walked out of the building in front of Evan and Bethany. She fired out of the Jeep like a cannonball, and he leaped out, hurrying to catch up. The crazy woman was going to get them shot.

The taller of the two men glanced at them and said something to the other cowboy who nodded and walked toward the barn. The tall man started toward them, a wide smile on his face. Evan couldn't help feeling a bit sorry for the guy, not knowing he was about to encounter a rabid she-bear. But then again, if he was guilty of the crimes committed at Moose Valley, he deserved Bethany's ire.

The man's smile dimmed as Bethany stalked toward him. Evan jogged up beside her and grabbed her arm. "Calm down, okay?"

She lanced him with a scathing glare and jerked away. With his hat on, the man stood more than a foot taller than Bethany, but somehow Evan felt the unsuspecting man had the disadvantage.

"I'm John Ogden, owner of this place. Can I help you with something?"

"Yeah, you can stop stealing our customers and pay for my dad's doctor bills." Bethany stomped right up to the man and halted, her chest heaving with rage.

Mr. Ogden darted a confused glance at Evan then refocused on Bethany as if he was afraid to take his eyes off her too long for fear of what she might do. *Wise man.*

"Excuse me?"

Evan stepped in front of Bethany and nearly looked the man eyeball to eyeball. She snorted and tried to squeeze past him. He elbowed her back. "We're from Moose Valley Ranch. Someone has been sabotaging the Schaffers' operation and causing all kinds of problems, as well as calling their booked guests and offering them a better deal to change wagon tours."

"I can talk for myself, Evan Parker."

Mr. Ogden scowled. "I resent the implications you're making. We run a clean operation here and have enough business that we don't have to steal from our neighbors."

"That's a lie."

The man narrowed his eyes at Bethany. "Now see here, ma'am. You can't come onto another man's property and call him a thieving scoundrel with no evidence."

Evan pulled her back and got in her face. "Let me handle this. You're too upset."

She pursed her lips like a woman sucking on a lemon and crossed her arms. "Fine."

Evan spun back around. "We have evidence." He pulled out his cell phone and showed the man his phone with the caller ID showing Ogden Outfitters.

The man lifted his brows and shook his head and crossed his arms, too. "So, you received a phone call from us. What does that prove?"

"The man who called offered me a special deal if I'd cancel my reservation with Moose Valley and sign up for a wagon tour here. He gave me a number to call him back." Evan pulled the paper from his pocket and handed it to Mr. Ogden.

The man's irritation immediately turned to shock, if his changing facial expressions were any indication. Evan knew he recognized the number.

Mr. Ogden sighed and stared toward the mountains. He ducked his head then finally looked back at them. "That's my son's cell phone."

Bethany stepped forward. "Is his name Ryan?"

"How did you know that?"

"He's dating a girl named Maggie, right?" Bethany's stance

seemed to relax now that they were getting some favorable responses.

"Yes, that's correct." John Ogden nodded.

"Well, Maggie used to work for us." Evan noticed she left off the part about Maggie being laid off.

"So. That doesn't prove anything." Mr. Ogden crumpled the paper in his fist.

"We think Maggie stole the names from our reservation file. Your son must have been the one to make the phone calls."

The man shook his head. "But why? We have plenty of business."

"Maybe you have plenty of business because of the people who came here instead of our ranch. Do you have any idea how much money in lost fees we're talking about? Tens of thousands of dollars, not to mention that whoever tampered with our equipment and supplies put people's lives in danger. My own dad is in the clinic right now with a concussion and broken wrist because of it. And if someone stole *our* guests, who's to say they didn't steal some from other ranches?"

Mr. Ogden blanched. "I can't believe Ryan is involved, but there's only one way to find out." He spun around and marched toward the barn. Instead of going inside, he bypassed the structure and strode out to a grove of pine trees where someone was waxing a shiny red convertible.

"Ryan Ogden, I presume." Evan hurried to keep up and held on to Bethany's arm to prevent her from running ahead.

"Let go of me," she hissed. "I want to be there when that man confronts his son."

"We're there." Evan hoped he never got on Bethany's bad side. It was a fierce thing to behold.

"This is your phone number, right, Ryan?" Mr. Ogden said as he handed the piece of paper to a handsome young man who looked about seventeen.

"Yeah, so what?" Ryan glanced at Evan and Bethany as they approached, then back at his father. He shifted from foot to foot, looking as if he was ready to bolt.

Evan moved closer, determined not to let the youth get away. He recognized the boy's voice from the phone. Bethany needed all this to be over so she could get on with her life.

"These folks say someone called and tried to get them to change their reservation from Moose Valley Ranch to ours. You wouldn't know anything about that, would you?"

Ryan's face paled, and he backed up against the car. "No, Dad. For real."

"Then why do they have your cell number? And how is Maggie involved?"

Ryan straightened, and a look of panic engulfed his face. "Maggie told? Why that. . ."

"So you were part of this?"

The tall teen shrugged. "I heard you talking on the phone. You said we might have to leave here if business didn't pick up. I was only trying to help."

John Ogden hung his head. "Did you also pull pranks on the wagon tours at the Moose Valley Ranch?"

"What pranks?"

Mr. Ogden looked at Evan, as if he hoped his son wasn't involved in that part of the situation.

"Tampering with the food, turning horses loose, letting air out of tires, and cutting harnesses on the wagons."

Mr. Ogden's eyes widened more with each item Evan rattled off.

"I didn't do those things, Dad. Really."

"Whoever did rides a horse with an egg bar shoe," Bethany said. "We found tracks."

Mr. Ogden ran his hand through his hair. "My son's horse

is the only one here that wears them. We recently bought the animal, and it already had those shoes."

"So," Ryan said, "lots of other horses around these parts wear them."

Bethany shook her head. "I've lived here my whole life and don't know another rancher who uses bar shoes. Face it, kid, you're busted."

"You don't have any proof that I did anything." He crossed his arms.

Evan pulled out his phone and showed Ryan his number. "I recognize your voice from when you called me earlier today."

"C'mon, Evan." Bethany grabbed his arm and tugged. Confused by her sudden desire to leave when they were making headway, he dug in his feet.

"You were right about coming here without the sheriff," she said. "Let's go to town and talk to him."

"No!" John and Ryan Ogden yelled at the same time.

The father removed his hat and scratched the top of his balding head. "What if we agree to pay for everything that was damaged and for your father's medical bills?"

Bethany crossed her arms. "That doesn't help us with the loss of income."

Mr. Ogden sighed. "I'd like to keep the law out of this, if possible. Ryan can sell his car and give you the money to make up for what you lost, if that's agreeable to you."

"Da—ad! You can't be serious. I paid for this car myself."

John Ogden lifted his chin. "You paid for it working for me at a ridiculous salary. You will sell it to make restitution to these people, and if that doesn't cover what they've lost, we'll sell your horse. Now get in the house before I do something I'll regret."

Evan watched the young man skulk toward the house. Calling the sheriff may have been the legal thing to do, but putting the young man in jail with truly hardened criminals wouldn't help him any.

"If you'll be so kind as to make a list of all the damages, medical bills, and lost income, I'll have my accountant cut you a check, and I'll deliver it myself." Mr. Ogden paused and took a deep breath. "I hope you will seriously consider not prosecuting my son. His mother died in a car accident when Ryan was learning to drive. He blames himself for her death. Coming here was a way for us to start over."

Bethany studied the ground, and Evan wondered if she'd cut the poor man some slack now that she knew he wasn't involved. Would she give Ryan some measure of grace since she herself knew what it was like to lose a mother?

She looked up. "I apologize for blaming you for our troubles, Mr. Ogden. My father was just hurt today, and I'm worried about him, but that's no excuse for the way I spoke to you."

"Don't worry about it. You had just cause. I'm sorry that we had to meet under these circumstances."

"Me, too. I'll have to discuss this with my father and see whether he wants to press charges against Ryan or Maggie."

Mr. Ogden nodded, shook Bethany's then Evan's hand, and they parted.

Evan guided Bethany back toward the Jeep.

"What a relief to have that over." She rolled her head and glanced up at Evan. "Thank you for being here with me and helping me keep a lid on my anger."

Evan hugged her. "Anytime."

He opened her door then walked around the front of the Jeep. Bethany's mouth moved, and he thought she mumbled something about him staying forever. He shook his head. Probably just wishful thinking on his part.

sixteen

Bethany fluffed the pillow and placed it under her dad's injured arm. "Anything else I can get for you before I go?"

"No. I'll just sit here in my recliner and rest for a while. Maybe watch some television later."

She patted his shoulder. "Okay. I left the bottle of pain pills there by your glass of water in case you need them."

"Thanks. I'm glad to have that mystery cleared up and for things to get back to normal. I'll call our lawyer tomorrow and see what he recommends."

Bethany nodded, wishing they could forget the whole ordeal but knowing they couldn't.

Her dad lifted his arm and winced. "This confounded cast is going to make things mighty hard for me."

She leaned down and kissed his leathery cheek. "You deserve a good rest, Dad. You work too hard as it is."

"I work hard because there's so much to do." He ran his good hand through his hair. He didn't show emotion often, and the look on his face now made Bethany realize how much her father had aged since she'd first gone off to college.

"You just rest and get better. I'll take care of your chores, and what I can't do, I'm sure Shep will be happy to help with."

"But you're going back to Denver soon. How will I manage without you?"

She scooted around the recliner and sat on the edge of the sofa, hating that her normally tough father sounded like a lost little boy. "I called my boss yesterday and told him that I couldn't take the job because I'm needed here."

Hope glistened in her dad's eyes. "You're staying? For how long?"

"Indefinitely. My boss needed someone for the position and said he was sorry but he couldn't hold it open any longer. He's hiring somebody else."

A muscle ticked in his jaw, and he looked away. "I'm sorry. I know how much you wanted to leave here and live in Denver."

Turning to face the big picture window, she stared at the mountains. The ones she could see looked gray because of the cloudy sky that threatened rain. The curtains fluttered at the open window, and a chilly breeze cooled the room. "I guess I just needed to grow up, Dad. This place is my heritage, and I need to be here to help you run things. Don't take me wrong." She grinned. "I don't care if I never go on another wagon tour, but I want to be here. Guess you might say I've grown up."

His warm smile stole away any apprehension that she was making a mistake. Maybe she could get him to start going to church with her one day.

He leaned back and closed his eyes. "I can't tell you what a relief that is."

She placed her hand over his. "There's nothing more important in this world than God and family. It just took me a while to realize that."

He grunted, but there was a hint of a smile on his lips. She stood, unfolded a light blanket, and laid it over him. "Get some rest, okay?"

He mumbled a thank-you.

Her hand was on the doorknob when he cleared his throat. "Have you got that computer all set up?"

"Yeah, it's up and running. Since you can't do much of your ranch work until you heal, you'll have more time to learn how to run it." She couldn't help grinning at his disinterested grunt.

"Let your young man know how much I appreciate his help, and if his family wants to come and take another tour, let them do it. No charge."

"He's not my young man, and I already made him that offer, but I don't think you have to worry about Evan taking us up on it."

"Why couldn't you fall in love with a cowpoke? And don't bother denying it; I was in love once...."

As his last words slurred, her breath froze in her lungs. Was it obvious to her dad that she'd lost her heart to Evan when it wasn't even clear to her?

She watched him, waiting for him to say more, but his lips fluttered with a heavy breath as sleep descended. She closed the door and stood in the hallway looking out the window. The views from their private quarters on the third floor were majestic, and she never tired of seeing them, but today her thoughts were on a certain man.

Did she actually love Evan? *Do I, Lord?*

Something inside her quickened, and she knew the truth in that instant. A silly grin tugged to her lips. She did love him!

She walked down the hall toward the stairs, amazed by the happiness she felt at that revelation. And if Evan loved her, they could work out their differences.

She had no clue how, but with God's help they could.

Feeling lighter than she had in years, Bethany wished she could slide down the banister like she had as a child. Instead, she trotted down two flights of stairs to the main floor of the lodge. She had to find Evan and talk with him—see if he felt anything for her.

No, she knew he did. It had been written on his handsome face and in his touch. He'd respected her choices enough that he hadn't forced his interest. And that made her love him more.

How was it that her love could be so strong now when an

hour ago she wasn't even aware of it? She shook her head, marveling at the mystery of it all.

Evan was leaving in the morning. She couldn't let him go without him knowing how she felt.

She checked the porch and noticed his laptop sitting there by itself. How odd. As protective as he was of his computer, she'd never seen him go off and leave it.

She scanned the area, and her gaze zeroed in on Evan's back where he stood in the parking lot. Her heart flip-flopped. He opened the door of a blue car and helped a woman out. She fell into his arms, and he held on, hugging her head to his chest.

Warning bells screamed in Bethany's head. *No! Not now.*

The hug went on entirely too long for the woman to be unimportant to him. Bethany's hopes and dreams plummeted like a stone kicked off a cliff. Evan kissed the woman's cheek.

Bethany grabbed the door frame. The back door opened, and a boy who looked ten or eleven climbed out. Evan released the woman and high-fived the boy, then wrapped him in a hug. Bethany held a hand to her heart.

Her first thought was to flee, but she had more faith in Evan than that. Curiosity propelled her out the front door and down the steps. Evan glanced in her direction and smiled. He released the boy and walked toward her. "Come and meet my sister and nephew."

She resisted closing her eyes in relief as he took her hand and pulled her toward his sister. The woman had the same blue eyes, but her hair was darker than Evan's.

"Erin, this is Bethany Schaffer. She and her dad own the ranch here. I've been helping her with some computer problems she's been having."

Erin nodded, but her gaze dropped to Evan's and Bethany's linked hands. One eyebrow lifted. Evan must have noticed, because he cleared his throat and turned loose of her.

"Nice to meet you, Miss Schaffer. It is Miss, isn't it?"

There was more to that question than was asked. Bethany smiled. "Yes, and it's a pleasure to meet you, too."

Evan clapped his hand on the boy's shoulder. "And this is my favorite nephew, Jamie."

"I'm your only nephew." The boy gave Evan a playful shove, and they pretended to be boxing with each other.

Erin shook her head. "I can't take those two anywhere."

Jamie jabbed at Evan, who dodged him then charged. The boy took off running with Evan close on his heels, and Bethany smiled at their silliness. Erin looked toward the corral, and Bethany noticed how much Taylor looked like her.

A sudden thought zinged its way through her mind. If things went well between her and Evan, this woman might one day be her sister-in-law.

Erin turned back to face Bethany. "Is Taylor around? I can't wait to see her. We've never been separated this long before. I probably should have just waited until Evan brought her home instead of driving all the way out here, but Jamie wanted to see the ranch."

"I'm sure Taylor missed you, too. She and Cheryl went riding, but they should be back soon." Bethany watched Evan and Jamie walk toward the corral. "She sure was a big help to Evan when he was sick."

Erin smiled. "That's good to know. She's a sweet girl but has had a hard time since her dad left." She looked toward the corral. "I don't know what I would have done without Evan being there to help me the past two years. We'd have never made it without him."

Bethany's heart felt as if a giant fist was squeezing it. In the past few weeks, she'd learned the value of family—of being there when your family needed you. If Evan loved her as much as she did him, it would mean he'd have to leave Laramie—have to leave his sister. How could she ask that of him when they obviously still needed him?

As if a bullet had hit her torso, a deep pain burned her heart. She couldn't. She had tried to run away from family and responsibility and couldn't ask Evan to do the same. She had to let him go.

A heaviness weighed down her spirit. Her lower lip quivered at the thought of losing him. She swallowed back a growing tightness in her throat. "It was nice to meet you, Erin, but I need to go tend to some things. Taylor should be back before too long."

Erin smiled again and waved good-bye then headed toward Evan and Jamie, who were coming back from the corral. Bethany spun and jogged up the stairs and into the lodge. She hurried around the counter and into the office, shutting and locking the door. Tears dripped down her chin and blurred her vision as she slumped to the floor.

She allowed herself time to cry, to grieve for what could have been. As the tears finally subsided, she remembered something her mother had told her: God knew what she was going through. No matter how bad the situation, the Lord was standing there with open arms to comfort her.

"Help me, heavenly Father. I'm sorry for doing things on my own for so long without leaning on You. I don't want to do that anymore."

She sniffled and rubbed her eyes.

"I don't know why You brought Evan here and let me fall in love if we can't be together. Help this pain in my heart to heal, and show me how to love Evan as a Christian brother.

"Please, Lord. Help me."

❧

Bethany opened the bathroom door and peeked both ways down the hall. She dashed toward the front foyer and peered around the corner. With the way clear, she hurried over to the registration desk and checked to see if anyone had left a message.

The loud buzz of conversation and clinking silverware echoed from the open doors of the dining hall. The spicy scent of seasoned chicken teased her senses, and her stomach complained that she'd skipped lunch, but she wasn't about to chance an encounter with Evan. If she could just stay out of his way for another fifteen hours, he'd be gone.

She jogged out the front door and to the barn. Her heart ached as if someone had yanked it out, tossed it onto the ground, and stampeded a herd of cattle over it. Unwanted tears stung her eyes and made her throat burn.

In the barn, she snatched up a curry comb and slipped into a stall. The black and white pinto turned from its feedbox to see who was there. "Hey, Patches. It's just me. How about a nice grooming?"

Pushing thoughts of Evan from her mind, she concentrated on trying to remember the words to a song she'd sung in church as a child. The tune was easy enough, but the words kept seeping from her mind like water through a colander.

She ran the curry comb over the horse's sleek hide and tried to remember the song again, but when the sentence ended in "heaven," the word reminded her of Evan. Her lip quivered and tears blurred her eyes. She rested her head against the horse's warm side. "How do I stop caring for him, Lord?"

Patches whickered, as if answering. Bethany wiped her moist eyes on her sleeve and resumed brushing the mare.

"So, there you are."

Lost in thought, she jumped at the nearness of Evan's voice. *Drat.* She'd let her guard down, and he'd found her. She ducked under Patches' chin and put the horse between herself and the man she was trying hard to forget.

"What's the matter, Bethany?"

She heard him shuffling his feet but didn't look at him. "Nothing. With Dad injured, I've just got extra work, that's all."

"There's more to it than that, isn't there?"

When she didn't answer, he moved along the stall gate as if trying to see her better.

"Come out here and talk with me. *Please.*"

She shook her head. "Can't. Got too much to do." An arrow of guilt stabbed her, but it was the truth. Her workload had doubled since her dad's injury.

Evan blew out a loud sigh. "You're going to make me come in there with that horse, aren't you?"

She ran the brush down the horse's withers. "Nobody's making you do anything."

"Fine." The latch rattled and the gate creaked as Evan swung it open then shut again.

Bethany seriously considered shinnying over the stall to get away from him, but Patches wasn't familiar with Evan, and she didn't want him or the horse getting hurt. She heard him back along the gate, no doubt never taking his eyes off the horse's hind end until he got to the side of the stall.

"The only thing worse than the front end of a horse is the back end." He uttered a nervous chuckle. He took the brush from her hand, set it down, then spun Bethany around to face him. "What's going on?"

She pursed her lips and looked up. The concern in his azure eyes stole her breath away. She had to be tough, or she just might confess her love for him. "Nothing."

His gaze clouded; then he had the audacity to grin. "You're not jealous because I'm spending time with my sister, are you?"

"What? No! Of course not."

Evan's right eyebrow lifted.

She wanted to punch that cocky look off his face, but

hurting a guest was against company policy. She scowled. "Why would I be jealous of your sister? I like Erin."

Patches swished her tail, and Evan dodged it. Bethany might have laughed if her heart hadn't been torn in two.

"Can't we talk out there?"

"There's nothing to talk about." She spun around, ready to flee, but he caught her upper arm. His touch sent quivers of fire shooting down to her fingertips. He turned her around to face him again.

"Bethany, I care about you. I want to know what's wrong." Evan cocked his head and studied her. He brushed a strand of hair from her cheek. "Tell me."

She shook her head. Evan sobered and took hold of her shoulders. Her mouth went dry at the intense look on his face.

"If you won't talk, then I have something I want to say. I can't leave without knowing where things stand between us. I don't want to just be friends. I want more."

She stared into his eyes, unable to catch her breath at the intensity in them.

He took her face in his hands; his palms warmed her ears and cheeks. "I may just be a geek from the city, but I love you, Bethany. If you feel the same, one way or another we can work things out between us, even if I have to move to Denver."

Hope washed through her. "I'm not going to Denver. I'm staying here. Dad needs me, and in a strange way, I think I need this place." She held her breath. Denver was one thing, but did her city boy love her enough to leave everything he knew and live on an isolated ranch? Would he leave his sister and her children to be here with her?

"But the big question is. . .do you need *me*?"

Without taking her eyes from his, she nodded. "I love you, too."

"Thank You, Lord!" He stared up at the ceiling as if God Himself were there. Finally, Evan sighed and looked back at her.

"But I can't ask you to leave Erin and the kids. They need you too much." Tears blurred her vision and slipped down her cheeks.

He dabbed at them with his thumbs. "I don't have all the answers, honey, but God does. We just need to ask Him to guide us. Can you trust Him with our future?"

Could she? Hadn't she just done that very thing a short while ago when she thought she'd lost Evan? Bethany nodded.

Evan pulled her close and leaned down, his soft lips touching hers. All her worries disappeared in that moment, and she returned his kiss.

Patches shifted and bumped into Bethany. Evan fell back against the wall of the stall, hugging her against him. He chuckled. "Can we please leave this horse pen now?"

Bethany rested her hand against his cheek. "It's called a stall, greenhorn, and you'd better get used to it."

epilogue

"You may now kiss your bride."

The pastor's word *bride* spun in Evan's head. *My bride. My wife.* Bethany waited, her deep brown eyes alight with love— for him. He wasn't about to disappoint her. Evan ducked his head and kissed his bride with all the promise of a lifetime of love to come.

The small group of friends and family gathered in the little church cheered and clapped.

"I'm pleased to introduce Mr. and Mrs. Evan Michael Parker."

Bethany held his arm, her whole face gleaming. Her father sat on the front row next to Elsie and Margaret, wiping his eyes with a hanky. Erin and the kids sat on the opposite row. Eager to have his wife alone for a moment, Evan led her down the short aisle toward the foyer at the front of the church. Behind him the pastor invited the guests to the reception at the ranch.

"Look, it's still snowing. I hope we don't get snowed in before we can leave on our honeymoon." Bethany stared outside then turned her concerned gaze on him.

"No worries today. It's our wedding day, and I'd like another kiss, Mrs. Parker. Quickly, before everyone else gets out here."

She cocked her head, looking so beautiful in her lacy white dress. "Oh, you would, huh?"

Still smiling, he claimed her lips until a woman behind him cleared her throat.

The Groovy Grannies stood side by side, both dressed in pink. Elsie stood on her tiptoes and patted his face. "I liked you from the moment we met."

"Same here." Evan kissed her cheek.

Margaret crossed her arms. "I still don't understand why you don't want to use our RV for your honeymoon. It has all the amenities you could want."

Evan resisted shuddering visibly at the thought of going anywhere in that bright pink monstrosity, but Bethany must have felt him tremble. She pinched the inside of his arm. "That's very kind of you, but we have other plans."

Elsie grinned. "I bet you're taking that bride of yours on a wagon train trip."

Everyone laughed at the horror that transformed Bethany's face. "Not in this lifetime. We're heading someplace warm, and that's all I'm saying."

Erin and the kids crowded in beside them. She leaned toward Bethany. "Welcome to the family."

"Thank you. I'm so glad to finally have a sister." The two women hugged.

"Does that mean I can call you 'Aunt Bethany' now?" Taylor asked.

Bethany smiled. "I guess it does."

"Sweet!"

"When do we get cake?" Jamie shifted from foot to foot, looking uncomfortable in his suit. Erin cut him a look, and he glanced down.

Evan hugged his nephew. "Soon, pardner."

The ranch hands muttered their congratulations and filed out to their pickups. Polly fluttered by, waving at them and dragging Cheryl with her. "I'll hug you at the ranch, but right now I've got to get back and keep those cowpokes out of the cake."

Evan wrapped his arm around Bethany, not willing to let

her get too far away. Soon he'd have her all to himself, but for now he had to share her.

"Evan, I saw a commercial on television advertising that video game you designed. You must be proud of your work."

Margaret smiled. "Isn't it exciting how God arranged things so you'd have a job that could be done anywhere?"

"Yeah, it is. I have to admit, I didn't see how things would work out, and I never imagined they'd hire me full-time, but God was always in control. I just wish Erin and the kids weren't going to be so far away." Evan hated leaving her alone, but God had made it clear that he was to move to the ranch.

Erin's bright smile made him wonder if she was keeping a secret.

Rob Schaffer handed the pastor an envelope and shook the man's hand. "Great wedding, Reverend. I hope you'll join us at the ranch for the reception."

The pastor nodded and smiled to someone waiting to talk with him. Evan's father-in-law joined the group. He smiled down at Bethany and then at Evan. "Mr. Ogden sent over a nice wedding present for you two."

"Really?" Bethany asked. "What is it?"

"Let's just say it's in the barn, and you'll probably get more enjoyment from it than your husband will."

Chuckles surrounded Evan, and he grinned.

"Whatever happened with that Ogden boy? I never got a chance to ask you." Margaret stared at Rob, who looked at Evan.

"Go on, son, you tell her."

"The judge gave Ryan and Maggie two hundred hours each of community service and sent them to a counselor. They've been helping out at the ranch every other Saturday to make restitution, and I've kind of taken Ryan under my wing, since he's a big computer fan."

Elsie clapped her hands. "That's wonderful."

"I have a surprise for you, too." Bethany's dad smiled and glanced at Erin. "Actually, *we* have a surprise. You want to tell him?"

Erin's eyes glimmered. "Mr. Schaffer offered me a job. I'm going to take Polly's place as the ranch cook. We're moving to the ranch, too!"

Evan's heart nearly burst, and he couldn't help letting out a whoop at the same time Taylor squealed and Jamie let out a "Woot!"

"That's the best news I've heard since Bethany agreed to marry me."

Suddenly Taylor sobered. "But what about the Wilkes family? They aren't leaving, are they?"

Evan knew what a blow it would be for Taylor to lose Cheryl as a friend. Without the girl's companionship, Taylor might not be so excited about moving.

Bethany grinned up at him. "Polly is pregnant. She's going to be helping with some of the new projects we're taking on and working the front desk."

"Now I don't have to mess with that crazy computer." Rob shook his head, and the group laughed.

Jingle bells sounded outside, and everyone turned their heads. The women gasped in unison as two white horses drawing a white sleigh decorated with red bows stopped outside the church.

Evan bowed at Bethany. "Your carriage awaits, milady."

Her wide smile was worth all the effort he'd gone to.

"I love it, but you can't seriously think we can ride all the way back to the ranch in that. It's freezing outside."

"How about just through town?"

Smiling, she grabbed his arm and pulled him toward the coat closet. He helped her into the long, hooded cloak Bethany had borrowed then slipped on his jacket. He was in for a big change, moving from the city to the country and getting married to the only girl he'd ever loved, but he was up for the challenge.

At the door, Evan picked up his bride and carried her to the sleigh, glad that the heavy snowfall had turned to light flurries. The sleigh's driver tipped his hat to them. Evan tucked his wife under a blanket. "Don't go anywhere."

He hugged his sister and shook his father-in-law's hand. "My SUV is parked where we agreed?"

Rob nodded and handed Evan his car keys. "See you two back at the ranch."

Jamie wadded up a snowball and tossed it at Evan. He jumped backward, right into one of the horses. The animal quivered and turned its head around, nipping at Evan. He dodged the big yellow teeth and leaped clear. His family hooted with laughter.

"C'mon, city boy. We have a reception to attend. Cake to cut. Presents to open."

Evan pressed his lips together. He was anxious to begin his life on the ranch with Bethany, but he'd be just as happy if he never saw another horse.

He climbed in beside his wife and scooted close against her, covering them both with the lap blanket.

Bethany was still giggling and shaking her head. "Whatever am I going to do with you?"

He grinned. "Kiss me, I guess."

A Letter To Our Readers

Dear Reader:

In order that we might better contribute to your reading enjoyment, we would appreciate your taking a few minutes to respond to the following questions. We welcome your comments and read each form and letter we receive. When completed, please return to the following:

Fiction Editor
Heartsong Presents
PO Box 719
Uhrichsville, Ohio 44683

1. Did you enjoy reading *A Wagonload of Trouble* by Vickie McDonough?
   ❑ Very much! I would like to see more books by this author!
   ❑ Moderately. I would have enjoyed it more if

   _____

   _____

   _____

2. Are you a member of **Heartsong Presents**? ❑ Yes ❑ No
   If no, where did you purchase this book? _____

   _____

3. How would you rate, on a scale from 1 (poor) to 5 (superior), the cover design? _____

4. On a scale from 1 (poor) to 10 (superior), please rate the following elements.

   ____ Heroine   ____ Plot
   ____ Hero   ____ Inspirational theme
   ____ Setting   ____ Secondary characters

5. These characters were special because? _____

_____

_____

6. How has this book inspired your life? _____

_____

_____

7. What settings would you like to see covered in future
   Heartsong Presents books? _____

_____

_____

8. What are some inspirational themes you would like to see
   treated in future books? _____

_____

_____

9. Would you be interested in reading other **Heartsong
   Presents** titles? ❏ Yes ❏ No

10. Please check your age range:
   ❏ Under 18   ❏ 18-24
   ❏ 25-34   ❏ 35-45
   ❏ 46-55   ❏ Over 55

Name _____

Occupation _____

Address _____

City, State, Zip_____

Montana Rose

Ride into this rocky, riveting romance, where a fragile and beautiful widow finds herself hitched to the wagon of a sod-busting stranger.

Contemporary, paperback, 320 pages, 5³⁄₁₆" x 8"

_____